P9-CLC-171

Gray Lockwood was a force to be reckoned with...

Gray was intelligent, observant, dynamic and demanding.

Blakely shouldn't be turned on by his confidence and domineering attitude. But she was. He watched her, his own gaze narrowed with wary curiosity. The moment stretched between them.

She breathed in the tantalizing scent that had been taunting her for days. *Him.*

"To hell with it," he finally murmured.

All the air whooshed out of Blakely's lungs as if he'd slammed her against the wall, although he hadn't. Heat flamed up her skin. His mouth dropped to hers. Her gasp of surprise backed into her lungs as he kissed her.

The first touch was light, but that didn't last long.

Seconds later, Gray was opening his lips, diving in and demanding everything from her.

His tongue tangled with hers, stroking and stoking and driving the need she'd been ignoring into a raging inferno...one she couldn't deny.

* * *

The Sinner's Secret by Kira Sinclair is part of the Bad Billionaires series.

Dear Reader,

One event can change the course of a life...a chance encounter, a family tragedy, being falsely accused of a crime. Often, those moments, good or bad, help shape who we are. Gray Lockwood understands this truth firsthand because, while being sent to prison wasn't what he ever would have wanted, the experience shaped him into the man he is: dedicated, honorable and hell-bent on finding the truth.

Blakely Whittaker understands, as well. She's spent her entire life trying to atone for her father's sins. She has a very strong sense of right and wrong, which made testifying against Gray easy when she uncovered evidence that he committed a crime. But now...he's back in her life. And she's starting to believe she might just have been wrong, about the crime and about him.

Sometimes, what we initially think is a setback can actually become one of the most defining moments of our life. I hope you enjoy reading Gray and Blakely's story! I'd love to hear from you at kirasinclair.com, or come chat with me on Twitter at Twitter.com/kirasinclair. And don't forget to check out the other Bad Billionaires books coming soon!

Best wishes,

Kira

3 1526 05460145 2

KIRA SINCLAIR

———

THE SINNER'S SECRET

HARLEQUIN
DESIRE

If you purchased this book without a cover you should be aware
that this book is stolen property. It was reported as "unsold and
destroyed" to the publisher, and neither the author nor the
publisher has received any payment for this "stripped book."

HARLEQUIN®
DESIRE™

Recycling programs
for this product may
not exist in your area.

ISBN-13: 978-1-335-20947-4

The Sinner's Secret

Copyright © 2020 by Kira Bazzel

All rights reserved. No part of this book may be used or reproduced in any
manner whatsoever without written permission except in the case of brief
quotations embodied in critical articles and reviews.

This is a work of fiction. Names, characters, places and incidents
are either the product of the author's imagination or are used fictitiously.
Any resemblance to actual persons, living or dead, businesses,
companies, events or locales is entirely coincidental.

This edition published by arrangement with Harlequin Books S.A.

For questions and comments about the quality of this book,
please contact us at CustomerService@Harlequin.com.

Harlequin Enterprises ULC
22 Adelaide St. West, 40th Floor
Toronto, Ontario M5H 4E3, Canada
www.Harlequin.com

Printed in U.S.A.

Kira Sinclair's first foray into writing romance was for a high school English assignment, and not even being forced to read the Scotland-set historical aloud to the class could dampen her enthusiasm...although it definitely made her blush. She sold her first book to Harlequin Blaze in 2007 and has enjoyed exploring relationships, falling in love and happily-ever-afters since. She lives in North Alabama with her two teenage daughters and their ever-entertaining bernedoodle puppy, Sadie. Kira loves to hear from readers at Kira@KiraSinclair.com.

Books by Kira Sinclair

Harlequin Desire

Bad Billionaires

The Rebel's Redemption
The Devil's Bargain
The Sinner's Secret

Harlequin Blaze

The Risk-Taker
She's No Angel
The Devil She Knows
Captivate Me
Testing the Limits
Bring Me to Life
Handle Me
Rescue Me

Visit her Author Profile page at Harlequin.com, or kirasinclair.com, for more titles.

You can also find Kira Sinclair on Facebook, along with other Harlequin Desire authors, at Facebook.com/harlequindesireauthors!

There would be no Bad Billionaires
without my amazing editor, Stacy Boyd.
She believed in me and this project
from the very beginning.
I'm grateful for her support, guidance and
vision that helped make this series amazing.
Thank you, Stacy!

One

The last two weeks had been surreal, culminating in this moment. Blakely Whittaker stood behind her new desk, staring at the persistent log-in screen waiting for her to input something on her standard-issue laptop.

She had no idea what to do next.

A box of personal belongings waited in her car, which was parked in the basement deck. There was a folder of HR paperwork that Becky had handed her after a quick tour of the building. Blakely should probably read it all.

But her body wouldn't move. Instead, her head kept swiveling between the closed door of her own private office and the huge windows at her back with a view of the city.

A far cry from the dingy, cramped cubicle she'd called home for the last few years.

The people here were so different, too. Everyone she'd encountered, from Finn DeLuca—the charismatic guy who'd approached her about the job—to the receptionist and HR staff had been upbeat, personable and genuinely happy. A huge shift from the depressed, downtrodden lot she'd been working with.

Sure, it was a nice change. One she'd desperately needed, along with the raise that came with her new position as lead accountant for Stone Surveillance.

But something about the whole thing felt off.

Which was why she was still standing, unwilling to take a seat in the very expensive and, no doubt, very comfortable chair waiting beside her.

Blakely could hear the voices in her head—sounding strangely like her parents—fighting like an angel and a devil. Her mother on one shoulder, wary, practical, cynical, warning her that if something looked too good to be true then it most likely was. And her father on the other, eternally optimistic, opportunistic and not to mention criminally inclined, telling her that if someone wanted to give her the world, it was her obligation to take it and run before they figured out their mistake.

Which left her stuck in the middle, a product of both and often paralyzed by indecision.

No, that wasn't true. The decision had already been made. She was here, in her new office, which meant the only path was forward. After pulling out the chair, Blakely dropped into it and let out a deep sigh when her assumptions were confirmed. The thing was real leather. Hell, her last chair squeaked every time she stood up and the underside of the cushion had been held together by duct tape. And not the cute, decorative kind.

Opening the manila folder, she began reading through the packet of information on company policies, leave accrual and insurance plans. She was halfway through when the door to her office opened.

She expected to see Becky walking back in to give her more information, or maybe IT bringing her log-in info so she could access her computer.

But that wasn't who'd come in.

Blakely's belly rolled and her skin flushed hot as she took in the man lounging, bigger than some Greek god, against the now-closed door. Unfortunately, no matter what she thought of him personally, her physical reaction to Gray Lockwood had always been the same. Immediate, overwhelming, bone-deep awareness.

Today, that familiar and unwanted response mixed with a healthy dose of "what the hell?"

Because the last person she expected to saunter into her brand-new office was the man she'd sent to prison eight years ago.

"Bastard."

Gray Lockwood had been called much worse in his life, and probably deserved it.

Hell, he deserved it today, although not for the reasons Blakely Whittaker assumed. She no doubt thought he was a bastard for the past, which he wasn't. He *was* a bastard for maneuvering her into a corner today, though. Unfortunately for her, she hadn't fully realized just how tight a space she was in.

But she was about to learn.

"Is that any way to greet your new boss?"

Incredulity, anger, resentment and, finally, understanding washed across Blakely's face. Gray wanted to be thrilled with the reality he'd just crashed down over her head—like the farce that had rained down over his, the one she'd been an integral part of.

But none of the satisfaction he'd expected materialized.

Dammit.

It was wholly inconvenient. Especially since he still wasn't certain whether Blakely had been an unwitting participant in the deception that had landed his ass in jail, or a willing partner in the fraud.

Eight years ago, he'd been aware of Blakely Whittaker. She was an employee at Lockwood Industries. He'd passed her in the halls a time or two. Seen her in meetings. Been attracted to her in the same distracted way he'd regarded most beautiful things in his life back then.

All that changed the day he sat across from her in a courtroom and listened as she systematically laid out the concrete evidence against him. Blakely had provided the prosecution with a smoking gun.

One he'd never pulled the trigger on. Although, he hadn't been able to prove that. Then.

He still couldn't prove that now, but he was bound

and determined to find a way to exonerate himself. It didn't matter that he'd already paid for a crime he never committed. He wanted to get back his good name and the life he'd had before.

And Blakely was going to help him do it, even if she wasn't aware that's why she'd been hired by Anderson Stone as the newest employee at Stone Surveillance.

Stone and Finn had both asked Gray why he was pursuing the investigation. He'd served his time for the embezzlement and was free to live his life. He had enough money in the bank to do anything he wanted—or nothing at all.

Before he'd been convicted, he hadn't given a damn about the family company. And, yes, it stung like hell that his family had disowned him. His father had barred him from Lockwood and refused to speak to him. His mother pretended she never had a son. But he'd learned to live with those facts.

Back then, he hadn't much cared what people thought of him. He'd been lazy, uncaring, spoiled and entitled. Prison had changed him. Connecting with Stone and Finn on the inside had changed him. Now, it bothered him that people whispered behind his back.

Mostly because he hadn't done a damn thing wrong. He might have been a bastard, but he was a law-abiding one.

Blakely shot up from the chair behind her desk. "I work for Anderson Stone and Finn DeLuca."

"No, you work for Stone Surveillance. Stone and

Finn are two of the three owners. I happen to be the third."

"No one told me that."

"Because they were instructed not to."

Blakely's mouth set into the straight, stubborn line he'd seen several times. She might be petite, gorgeous and blonde, but she could be a pit bull when she wanted to be. He'd seen her determination firsthand. And not just in the courtroom, when she'd hammered the last nail in his coffin.

He'd watched her in meetings, impassioned about some piece of information she felt to be important. The way her skin flushed pink and her eyes flashed... Gorgeous, enticing and entertaining.

But she was also the kind of woman who placed that same passion into everything. And back then, Gray had been too lazy to want to take on that kind of intensity.

He'd appreciated it from afar, though.

Reaching into a drawer, Blakely pulled out her purse and looped the strap over her shoulder. "Why would you hire me? You hate me."

Gray shook his head, a half smile tugging at his lips. "*Hate* is such a strong word."

"I helped put you in prison. *Hate*'s probably the correct word."

"I wouldn't stake my life on it." Because as much as he wanted to hate the woman standing just feet away from him, he couldn't seem to do it.

Oh, sure, she was an easy target for all of his blame. And, it was still possible—no, probable—

that she was up to her eyeballs in the mess that had taken him down. But he wasn't going to learn the truth without her. And she wasn't likely to help him if she thought he blamed her.

"No? What word would you use then?"

Gray tipped his head sideways and studied her for several seconds. "I'll admit, you're not my favorite person. However, I'm not sure you deserve my hate any more than I deserved to be sent to prison."

Blakely scoffed. The sound scraped down his spine, but her reaction wasn't unexpected.

Shaking her head, Blakely scooted around her desk and headed for the doorway. Gray shifted, moving his body between her and the exit.

She stopped abruptly, trying to avoid touching him. Gray didn't miss the way she flinched. Or the way her hand tightened over the strap of her purse.

Smart woman.

Gray had spent the last several years biding his time. Not to mention beating other prisoners in an underground fighting ring that Stone, Finn and he had built. He'd needed a physical outlet, one that didn't constantly land him in solitary.

Those fights had taught him to measure and watch his opponents. To pick up on the subtle physical cues that telegraphed a thought before it became action.

Although, Blakely's intentions were far from subtle. She wanted out of this room and away from him.

Too bad for her.

They were going to be spending a lot of time together in the coming weeks.

"Get out of my way."

The way her eyes flashed fire caused an answering heat that sparked in the pit of Gray's belly. There was something enticing and intriguing about her show of bravado. Even if he didn't want to be impressed.

Gray let his lips roll up into a predatory smile. His gaze swept down her body. It was damn hard not to take in the tempting curves. The way her skirt clung to her pert ass and how the jacket she'd paired it with cinched in at her tiny waist.

A part of him wanted to refuse. To see what she'd do if he pushed a few buttons. Would she put her hands on him? Would his body react with a physical rush at the contact?

Not smart to play that game. Instead of standing his ground, Gray slid sideways, clearing a path for her to exit.

Because he didn't need his body to stop her.

"You're welcome to leave anytime, Blakely."

Her eyes narrowed as she watched him. "Thank… you," she said, her words slow, as if she was sensing danger, but was clearly unable to identify the jaws of the trap.

He let her get one step forward before he hit the pin.

"Although, it isn't like you have anywhere to go. I've taken the liberty of informing your former employer of some questionable activity I recently discovered."

"What questionable activity? I've done nothing questionable."

"Of course you haven't, but that's not what the evidence suggests."

Blakely sputtered, her mouth opening and closing several times before she finally whispered, "Bastard."

"You've already said that. Doesn't feel real great to have lies used against you, huh? Either way, you have no job to go back to. And we both know how difficult it was to find that one after being released from Lockwood."

Blakely's skin flushed hot and her ice-blue eyes practically glowed with fury. God, she was gorgeous when she was pissed.

"What do you want?" she growled. "Is this payback?"

In an effort to keep from doing something stupid, Gray crossed his arms over his chest. "Hardly. I want your help in proving my innocence."

"I can't do that."

"Because you're unwilling?"

Her voice rose in frustration. "No, because you're hardly innocent."

"Maybe you're wrong, Blakely. Have you considered that at all?"

"Of course I have," she yelled, leaning forward and punctuating the words with indignation. "Do you know how many nights I've lain awake, wondering? But I'm not wrong. The numbers and evidence don't lie. I saw proof, with my own eyes, that you embezzled millions of dollars from Lockwood's accounts."

"You saw what someone wanted you to see." Or what she'd maneuvered so that everyone else would see.

"I'm leaving. I'll find another job."

"Sure you will...eventually. But the question is, will you find it here in Charleston or in time to pay your sister's tuition? Or cover the mortgage payment for your mom? Or, hell, your own car payment? It's a little difficult to get a job if you can't drive to an interview."

"Bastard."

"Maybe you should invest in a thesaurus. The job here is real, Blakely. And despite everything, I'm fully aware that you're an excellent accountant. We want you to work for the company. We simply want you to accept another assignment before you begin that work. And we'll pay you handsomely for both."

"For how long?"

"What?"

"How long do I have to work at proving your innocence? Because I think this could turn into a never-ending story."

Gray watched her. It wasn't an unfathomable request. In fact, Finn had asked him much the same question. How long was Gray willing to put his entire life on hold to chase a ghost of a possibility?

"Six weeks."

Blakely growled in the back of her throat. Scrunched her nose up in distaste. And then said, "Fine," before walking out.

Blakely had no idea where she was going...but she needed to get away from Gray before she did something stupid.

Like start to believe him.

Or worse, give in to the invisible tether that pulled her to him whenever the man walked into a room.

The ladies' room down the hall offered her an escape.

The man was walking, talking sin. And always had been. He'd carried the reputation of being hell-bent on pleasure for pleasure's sake. Sex, adrenaline, fast cars and the jet-setting lifestyle.

Gray Lockwood's picture would appear next to the word *sinner* in the dictionary.

Seriously, it wasn't fair. The man had hit the lottery when he'd been born. And not just because he'd been part of a prominent Southern family with good breeding and lots of money. His parents had passed on some amazing genes.

The man was gorgeous, and he knew it. Eight years ago, the most important decision she'd ever seen Gray make was choosing which of the women throwing themselves at him that he would take to bed. He had a confident demeanor, an outgoing attitude and Greek-god good looks.

Sure, Blakely had found him attractive, as did every other female in his vicinity. But he'd been easy to resist because he'd been ungrounded, spoiled and entitled. The man had thrown around money like he was playing *Monopoly*. He had a reputation for buying expensive cars just to drive them fast and crash them. He'd loved to party and had been known for paying for twenty people to have a wicked week in Vegas or Monaco or Thailand. And during the trial, the prosecution had brought into evidence that he'd racked up millions in gambling debts.

Now, he was…different.

The beautiful body had been hardened, probably by some time in the prison gym if she had to guess. And she'd been hard-pressed to miss the puckered skin of a scar running down his left eyebrow into the corner of his deep green eye. Somehow, the imperfection made him even more appealing. Before, Gray Lockwood had been too perfect.

But the biggest change was in his demeanor. While he still had the ability to command any room he walked into, his force was quieter.

The question was, could she work with him for the next six weeks without either wanting to kill him or being tempted to run her hands down his solid body? Or, even more, could she work on a project she didn't believe in simply for money?

She had no doubt, then and now, Gray Lockwood had plenty of secrets to hide. She'd uncovered one and it had derailed her life. Did she really want to risk uncovering more?

Blakely groaned, rubbing her hands down her face before washing them. Leaning over the sink, she stared hard into her own reflection. She'd spent her entire adult life doing the right thing. Because integrity was important to her. As someone raised by a criminal and con artist…you either joined the family business or became straighter than an arrow.

Watching her father bounce in and out of jail her entire childhood, that decision had been a no-brainer.

She despised people who took the easy way out—anyone who took advantage of others' weaknesses or misfortunes. As far as she was concerned, Gray Lockwood was the worst kind of criminal.

Because he hadn't needed the money he'd embezzled.

Sure, he'd owed some nasty bookie a few million. But his net worth had been close to a billion. A lot of that wealth had been tied up in assets, but instead of liquidating, he'd decided to dip his hands into the family cookie jar. Probably because the spoiled rich boy thought he'd been entitled to it.

He'd never understood how taking that money had jeopardized the financial position of the company, not to mention the livelihood of all Lockwood Industries employees.

So the question was, could she spend the next six weeks pretending to work on a project she really didn't believe in, in exchange for a salary that she desperately needed?

A knot formed in the pit of her belly. It wasn't like she was lying to Gray. He knew full well she didn't believe him. He had to be aware she wouldn't exactly be the most motivated employee. Not to mention, he'd obviously maneuvered her here—which was something she'd have to talk with Anderson Stone and Finn DeLuca about, the assholes. So, really, she didn't owe Gray anything.

At the end of the day, the question was, could she go to sleep at night with a clear conscience if she stayed?

Today, the answer was yes. She might not like where she was standing, but she had no doubt Gray had backed up his statement and she'd have a hard time finding another job right now. He couldn't black-ball her with every company in the country, so eventually she'd find something. But that might entail uprooting her life and moving. And while that didn't necessarily bother her, she couldn't do it right now.

Not when she was concerned her father was back to his old habits.

God, how had her life come to this?

Taking a deep breath, Blakely straightened her spine. She'd stay, take Gray's money and work the six weeks. At least that would give her a cushion to line up something else.

She pulled out a paper towel and dried her hands, then pushed open the door. Two strides out, she jolted to a stop.

She didn't even need to turn her head to know he was there. Her entire body reacted, a riot of energy crackling across her skin. So inconvenient.

Slowly, she turned her head, anyway. Arms crossed over his chest, Gray leaned casually against the wall right between the doors to the restrooms.

"Feel better now?"

Two

Blakely watched him with wary eyes. "No, not really."

He shrugged, dismissing her statement. Because it didn't matter. He wasn't really worried about her comfort.

"Follow me," he said, pushing off from the wall and striding past her. Her tempting scent slammed into him—it was something soft and subtle, but entirely her. Gray remembered it from before.

The one time he'd gotten close enough to pull her enticing scent deep into his lungs had involved a clash in the break room over some creamer he'd "borrowed" from her. After that, he'd purposely kept his distance. She was a vixen, and he'd had to fight the urge to shut down her tirade by kissing the hell out of her. Not smart.

Blakely might be beautiful, but she had a remote, standoffish manner about her. She'd been cordial with her coworkers, but not overly friendly. She wasn't one of the women invited to a girls' night out after work. Everyone appreciated her dedication. However, she didn't exactly give off warmth.

And back then, Gray hadn't just been looking for warm, he'd been looking for red-hot. With no strings. Everything about Blakely screamed serious.

So it hadn't mattered that he couldn't keep his gaze from tracking her whenever she walked down the hallways. Or that he would fall asleep with the phantom scent of her tickling his nose if they'd passed in the lobby.

Hell, he needed to get his head back in the game. Because now, Gray wasn't so certain that the wall she'd put up between herself and everyone else wasn't to hide her own nefarious intentions.

At the end of the hallway, Gray paused. He waited for her to decide what she was going to do. When the click of her heels sounded against the marble floor, he continued to the right.

"Where are we going?" she asked from several paces behind, in no hurry to catch up once she'd made her decision.

Without turning around, he answered, "I've got all the records from my trial in another office. You're going to walk me through the evidence you presented against me."

"Why? You were there in the courtroom."

Yes, he had been. Watching her every move. The way she'd tucked a golden strand of hair behind her ear each time she looked down at the documentation the prosecution was using against him. Or how the sharp tip of her pink tongue would swipe across her lips each time she needed to pause and gather her thoughts before answering.

Had those pauses been her organizing thoughts, or her making certain she told the right lies?

Turning into the empty office beside hers, Gray waited until she brushed past him, then closed the door. "I sure was, but I didn't know then what I know now."

"And what do you know now?"

Oh, there were so many answers to that question. Most she wouldn't understand or appreciate. Several he had no intention of sharing with anyone, ever. But the only answer he was willing to give her right now was "Let's just say I used my time in prison to broaden my education."

Blakely made a buzzing noise in the back of her throat. "You're one of those."

"One of what?"

"People who go to jail and use the taxpayers' money to get an education they couldn't otherwise afford."

Wasn't that rich. "We both know I could—and did—afford a rather expensive Ivy League education before going to prison." He'd graduated from Harvard Business School. Sure, he'd barely made the cut and hadn't taken any of his classes seriously, but he had the damn degree.

"Little good it did you."

He wasn't going to refute that statement, mostly because he couldn't. "But, considering I'm innocent of the crime I was charged with and spent seven years imprisoned against my will because of it, the least the state owed me was an education in whatever I wanted."

"And what education was that?"

"I got a law degree."

"Of course you did."

At first, his plan was to figure out how to use his degree to help his own cause. Not surprising. However, it became obvious there wasn't much the legal system could do for him. His own attorneys filed every appeal possible, but they were all denied. Short of a call from the governor—not likely since the man had never liked Gray's father—that avenue wasn't going to help.

What he had used it for, though, was helping several of the inmates incarcerated with Stone, Finn and himself. Guys who might have been guilty, but had gotten screwed over or railroaded because they couldn't afford competent representation.

"That wasn't all I accomplished inside."

Blakely crossed her arms, her ice-blue eyes scraping up and down his body. "Oh, obviously."

Gray's lips twitched at her reaction. Her disdain was loud and clear. However, that didn't prevent heat from creeping into her cheeks or her nipples from peaking and pressing against the soft material of her shirt.

He wasn't stupid or oblivious to how women responded to him. He'd simply stopped taking advantage of the ones who shamelessly threw themselves at him. Funny how going without sex for seven years could make you appreciate it even more than having orgasms every day.

But he had no problem giving Blakely a hard time about her reaction. "And what, exactly, do you mean by that, Ms. Whittaker?"

"You know."

Gray hummed, drawing out the low, slow sound. "No, I don't think I do."

Blakely rolled her eyes, then pursed her lips and glared at him. Gray waited, silent, his gaze boring into hers. So he was being slightly juvenile by enjoying the way she shifted uncomfortably under his scrutiny.

Finally, she answered, as he'd known she would if he waited long enough. "It's clear you hit the gym whenever you could."

"How is that?"

She waved her hand in front of him. "You're huge. Broader, more muscular, than you were before."

"I didn't realize you'd noticed my physique before."

The heat in her cheeks deepened. "You made damn sure every woman at Lockwood noticed you. You wallowed in the attention from every female you could snag."

"But not you."

"No, not me."

"Is that because you weren't interested or because I didn't indicate that I was?"

Blakely's jaw clenched and her molars ground together. He could practically hear the enamel cracking from here. This was fun, but not very productive for the work he needed to get out of her. He could hardly expect her to be cooperative if he kept taking digs.

Shaking his head, Gray moved farther into the room. "I'm sorry, that wasn't very professional of me."

"No, it wasn't," Blakely quickly agreed.

"Let's agree that whatever concerns or animosity we had in the past, we both need to set them aside in order to work together right now."

Her eyes narrowed. She was damn smart and had no doubt picked up on the fact that he'd suggested they set them aside, not let them go. He wasn't ready to do that, not while he still questioned her role in the whole mess. Just as she wasn't likely to forget what she knew—or thought she knew—about him.

"Let's pretend we don't know anything about each other and start from square one."

She mumbled something under her breath that sounded suspiciously like "not likely." Gray decided to ignore it.

Pointing to a tower of seven cardboard boxes stacked in the corner of the room, he said, "Here's the data. I also have most of the files electronically, but we need any notes from the attorneys, as well.

Why don't we start by tackling the information you presented on the stand and go from there?"

They'd started three days ago by going over the accounting records the prosecution had entered into evidence. The information she'd uncovered showed a pattern of behavior that had gone undetected for several months. Small amounts had been withdrawn daily from the operating accounts and transferred to a holding account. The amounts had been strategic, varied and below any threshold for automatic review or audit. The final two transactions were transfers of funds out of the company and into offshore accounts.

That first withdrawal was what had finally flagged Blakely's attention. Unfortunately, not until almost four weeks later, when she'd been performing her monthly audit.

The first twenty-million-dollar transfer to Gray's account had been flagged immediately since none of the proper paperwork had been completed. However, considering who was involved, Blakely just assumed he'd failed to follow protocol. At first. Once she'd started digging, she'd discovered a second transaction.

That transfer out had been different. On the surface, it had looked legitimate, with the proper documentation and supporting paperwork in the electronic files. But something about it had still felt wrong. Being a huge international organization, she wasn't always privy ahead of time to large transactions...but more often than not she was aware when the company made large lump-sum purchases.

If anyone else had been auditing, they might not have bothered to look deeper. But she hadn't been willing to let it go. It had taken her a while to pull the threads of the transactions to figure out what had really happened—and that the two transactions were connected.

What she hadn't understood then, and still didn't understand, was why Gray had covered his tracks on one withdrawal but not the other. It made no sense. Unless you took into consideration how lazy the man was. Maybe he just assumed no one would question his actions.

Blakely hadn't been impressed with Gray's work ethic and didn't care whose son he was. The man had stolen millions of dollars from the company. Money they hadn't been able to afford to lose.

She'd turned over the information, never realizing just how instrumental she'd become in the trial process. She'd been inside plenty of courtrooms in her life, all for her father. None of the experiences had been pleasant and neither was Gray's trial. She'd been nervous on the stand, not because she hadn't been confident about the information, but because she'd hated being the center of attention.

Reviewing the documents now brought back all of those emotions. She'd been on edge for days and it was wearing on her.

Or maybe that was being cooped up in an office with Gray. Any other time, she would have said the office was pretty spacious, but put a sexy six-foot-two, two-hundred-and-twenty-pound guy in there, too, and it turned into a closet with all the air vacuumed out.

Letting out a frustrated groan, Gray tossed a bound testimony transcript toward an open box. The sheaf of papers bounced off the edge and clattered to the floor. "I need a break."

Amen. "Okay," Blakely said, seriously hoping he'd leave for a while. Or the rest of the afternoon. Or the week.

Standing up, he put his hands at the small of his back and leaned backward. The audible pop of his spine made Blakely shiver.

She tried to concentrate on the report in front of her. But it was damn hard not to notice every move he made. Each time Gray passed behind her chair, the tension in her body ratcheted higher. Her neck and shoulders ached with the struggle to ignore the physical awareness she really didn't want. Without thought, Blakely reached around and began pinching the muscles running up into her neck, hoping the knots would loosen.

They were starting to…until Gray brushed her hands out of the way and took over. The minute his grip settled onto her shoulders, Blakely bolted upright in her chair.

"Easy," he murmured. "Is this okay?"

Was it? Heat seeped into her skin. Her body tingled where he touched. Logically, Blakely knew she should say no. Move away. But she didn't want to and somehow found herself slowly nodding.

Gray's fingers dug deep into her muscles. At first, what he was doing hurt like hell…until her muscles started to relax and let go. Then it felt amazing.

Blakely was powerless to stop herself from melting beneath Gray's touch. Delicious heat spread from his fingers, down her shoulders and into her belly. A deep sigh leaked through her parted lips as she sagged against the back of her chair.

"God, you're so uptight."

"Don't ruin this," she groused.

"Admit it. You wouldn't know how to relax if someone gave you a flowchart."

"And you know nothing except how to relax."

Gray let out an incredulous chuckle, his grip on her shoulders tightening for a split second. "You know nothing about me." Then he dropped his hands.

Blakely bit back a cry of protest. Nope, she refused to beg him to touch her.

Scooting around her, Gray headed for the door. "I'm gonna go grab something to eat. Want me to get you something?"

It was well past lunchtime, but she'd been nose-deep in the report and hadn't noticed until now. At Gray's prompting, her stomach let out a growl loud enough for them both to hear.

A teasing smile tugged at the corners of his mouth. "I'll take that as a yes."

He was out the door before Blakely could tell him not to bother. Shrugging, she let him go, grateful for the reprieve so she could get herself back under control.

* * *

He'd needed to get out of there.

Never in his life had he gotten so hard from merely touching a woman's shoulders. Although, if he was going to be honest, his physical reaction to Blakely had little to do with actually touching her skin.

It had more to do with the way she'd softened beneath his hands. The way she'd relaxed, letting her head loll back against his belly. The soft sigh of pleasure and relief she'd made in the back of her throat. The way her eyes had slowly closed, as if savoring the sensations he was giving her.

If he hadn't left, he was going to embarrass himself. Or embarrass them both when she noticed his reaction. Food had been a quick, easy excuse.

He was two steps past Stone's office when his friend called out, "Gray."

He backed up, then pivoted inside.

"How's it going?"

There was no need to wonder what Stone was asking about. The only case Gray was working on right now was his own. "Nowhere."

"I'm sorry, man. Is she cooperating?"

"Yeah." At first, Blakely had appeared to be shuffling papers around more than looking at them. But it hadn't taken her long to actually start reading and digging, which didn't surprise him. Blakely was the kind of woman who couldn't ignore a task once it was placed in front of her. She worked hard and did her absolute best no matter what.

"What are you going to do if there's nothing to find there?"

"Honestly? I have no idea. I mean, it's likely the files won't give us anything, but I have to look, anyway."

"I don't blame you."

"Joker's working his magic, too. Maybe he'll find something."

Their freelance hacker was one of the best on the east coast. Gray had cultivated an introduction through one of the guys he'd fought on the inside. He made damn sure not to ask what else Joker was working on because he didn't want to know. The guy had a reputation for being choosy about his projects and difficult to find.

"We can hope. Let me know if there's anything Finn or I can do."

Stone's offer was unnecessary since Gray already knew the two men would do anything he needed without question. But it was nice to hear, anyway. Especially when he had no one else in his corner.

"Thanks, man," he said, starting to back out of the office.

"A little advice?"

Gray paused, tilting his head and eyeing his friend.

"Don't be a dick," Stone said.

"What?"

His eyebrows rose. "She's gorgeous and I can practically see the sparks you two are striking from my office. You've spent too much time getting her here to screw it up simply because you haven't gotten laid since you've been out."

"I've gotten laid." Okay, that wasn't true. But he wasn't about to admit that to Stone, who'd just give him hell over the fact. Sex wasn't exactly high on his priority list right now. He couldn't move on with his life until he figured out just who had screwed him over. And why.

Because there was no way of knowing when or if it would happen again until he did.

"Not nearly enough."

"I wasn't aware there was an orgasm quota I needed to fill. Perhaps you should put that in my personal development plan."

"Asshole," Stone countered, no heat behind the word.

He was about to make another snide comment when a commotion sounded down the hall.

"Sir, you can't just walk back there," Amanda, their receptionist, hollered down the hall.

Both men headed straight for the doorway. Gray hit it first, fists balled at his sides, his body strung and ready for a fight. Stone was right behind him, no doubt also prepared.

Several of their employees crowded into the hallway, but Gray and Stone both started telling them to get back into their offices and lock their doors. Considering their line of business, it paid to be careful. It wasn't that long ago that Piper, Stone's wife, had been kidnapped and held against her will.

Halfway down the hall, Amanda was chasing after

a man stalking down the line of offices. "I'm just looking for my daughter. I know she's here."

"Sir, if you tell me who she is, I'll be happy to get her for you."

The gentleman waved his hand, dismissing Amanda. "I don't have time for that. They'll be right behind me."

From behind, the man appeared disheveled. Although his clothes were obviously of good quality, his shirt had come untucked from his slacks, the tail of it hanging down past the bottom of his suit coat. The hems of his pants were splotchy with mud and water.

It had been raining earlier in the day, but had stopped several hours ago. However, this guy looked like he'd been tromping through mud puddles and fields.

It didn't take long for Gray to catch up to Amanda. Wrapping a hand around her arm, he pulled her to a stop. "I've got it from here."

"Sir, *who's* going to be right behind you?" Gray asked, his deep voice loud as it echoed against the hallway walls.

The guy glanced over his shoulder, but shook his head instead of answering.

"Who are you looking for?"

"I've already said—my daughter."

At that moment, the office door at the end of the hall, the one he and Blakely had been using for the past several days, swung open. Blakely stepped straight into the path of the man.

Gray cursed under his breath and sped up. He

didn't think this guy was dangerous—he didn't appear to be holding a weapon or have one tucked into a holster anywhere on his body—but Gray really had no desire to test that theory with Blakely's safety.

"Get back inside," he said at the exact same time Blakely said, "Dad?"

Three

Oh, God. What was her father doing here? Blakely wanted to scream or curse or both.

"Dad?" Gray's dark, smoky voice floated to her from down the hall. Squeezing her eyes shut, Blakely prayed for strength. And wished her face wasn't currently going up in flames. Which it obviously was, since her cheeks felt like they were on fire.

Of course, he would be right there to witness her father at his absolute worst. She was never going to live this down.

"Baby girl, I don't have much time." Her father was completely oblivious to the people hovering in the hallway, gawking at the spectacle he was making. Or, more likely, he just didn't give a damn.

Her father had never cared what kind of stir he

left in his wake, or whether it bothered the people closest to him.

Blakely threw a glance toward Gray, who'd stopped several feet away, hands balled into fists on his hips and the fiercest scowl scrunching up his handsome face. An unwanted thrill shot through her system. There was something attractive about him, like he'd come ready to swoop in and save her.

Yeah, right.

Not wanting to deal with that thought, Blakely's gaze skipped down to Stone, who was lingering behind Gray, a quizzical expression on his face. She didn't have time to handle either of them right now. Not with her father spouting gibberish.

"Much time before what?" she asked, directing her attention back to her father.

"Before the authorities arrive to arrest me."

Damn, it was worse than she'd thought. *"Dad."*

"I didn't do it."

If she had a dollar for every time she'd heard that… "Uh-huh. What are you being arrested for this time?"

"Conspiracy to commit murder."

Blakely blinked. Her mind blanked. Everything went silent for several seconds before a roar of sound rushed through her. "Excuse me?"

Her dad was a lot of things. A con artist, an idiot, a dreamer and a thief. What he wasn't was a murderer.

"I'm being framed for this. But there's not enough time to explain. I need you to get in touch with Ryan and tell him to come fix it."

Blakely bit back a groan. If she ever heard that

name again, it would be too soon. Ryan O'Sullivan had been part of her life since the day she was born… and a thorn in her side for just as long.

"Dad, you promised."

The hangdog expression on her father's face didn't make the pang in her stomach ease any. She was seriously tired of feeling like the parent in their relationship, especially when he gave her that misbehaving, little-boy-caught-with-his-hand-in-the-cookie-jar expression.

Life wasn't supposed to be like this.

"He's my best friend, pet. What was I supposed to do?"

"Stay away from the man who is single-handedly responsible for landing you in prison several times." It appeared, despite everything she'd done to stop the cycle, the man was going to have a hand in sending her father right back. "We agreed when you got out that you were going to cut all ties with Ryan O'Sullivan."

"I tried."

Blakely was quite familiar with the obstinate set of Martin Whittaker's jaw. She wanted to scream. And cry. But neither reaction would help the situation.

"Not hard enough, and now look at what's happening." Blakely flung her hands wide to encompass the Stone Surveillance offices. Other people were now sticking their heads into the hallways to eavesdrop on the juicy gossip.

Wonderful. She might not be thrilled to be working here, but that didn't mean she wanted her family's dirty laundry aired for everyone to judge. "This is where I work, Dad."

Martin let out a sigh and stepped closer, the petulant expression morphing into true regret.

Dammit. That was always how he got her. If there was a single shred of hope, Blakely just couldn't turn her back on him. Her mother and sister both called her ten kinds of a fool. And a softy.

She was probably both.

But when Martin reached for her, Blakely couldn't force herself to stop him. Although, she didn't hug him back. This wasn't the kind of problem that could be solved with some trite Irish quip and a pat on the head.

"I didn't do this, Blakely," he murmured. "I promise. Please, just contact Ryan. He'll take care of everything."

Sure. She wouldn't call that man if he was the sole survivor of the apocalypse. Instead, Blakely started mentally flipping through names of good attorneys. She didn't know many. Her father hadn't ever been able to afford representation, so he'd always stuck with whomever the court appointed. But this time, thanks to Gray and his maneuvering, she had the means to pay for someone who might actually be able to help.

Although, she couldn't quite shake the feeling that it wouldn't make a difference. Her father might not think he was guilty of anything, but that didn't mean he wasn't guilty in the eyes of the law. Especially with a charge like conspiracy.

Who the heck could he have been accused of trying to kill?

Blakely shook her head. One issue at a time.

Before she could open her mouth and ask, another commotion started at the end of the hall. Two officers were stalking toward them, followed by Amanda. They didn't have their guns drawn, but their hands were on the butts ready to pull at the first sign of concern.

In a loud, stern voice, one of the officers demanded, "Mr. Whittaker, put your hands in the air."

Slowly, her father's arms rose over his head. Staring straight at her, his soft blue eyes filled with regret and remorse.

Blakely's throat grew tight and a lump formed. Her body went ice-cold with fear, sadness and frustration.

There was nothing she could do but watch.

One of the officers took another step down the hallway, but before he could reach her father something unexpected happened. Gray moved between them, blocking his path.

"What is Mr. Whittaker being charged with?"

The officer's gaze narrowed. His eyes raked up and down Gray, sizing him up. But that didn't seem to bother Gray. He was perfectly relaxed, his body loose and hands open by his sides.

"Conspiracy to commit murder."

Hearing the words from her father had already sent a shock wave through Blakely. But hearing them from an officer, hand poised on a gun, made her downright terrified.

Because her father wasn't known for being smart or cooperative.

"Now, please step out of the way."

Gray stood exactly where he was, feet unmoving, for what felt like forever. The hallway was silent, the only sound the whoosh of air through the vents in the building. Everyone waited.

Her father was connected to one of the most notorious crime families in Charleston.

Everyone knew Ryan O'Sullivan, mostly because he was the kind of man you wanted to avoid, if at all possible. At least if you were a law-abiding citizen.

There was a time in his life when Gray would have avoided any association with the man. But now... O'Sullivan didn't scare him. He might have connections, but then, so did Gray.

He'd never had any personal experience with the man, or any of his associates. However, the minute they were done here, he'd be making a few phone calls because he was absolutely certain one of his contacts knew O'Sullivan.

And while information on Martin Whittaker might be interesting, what he really wanted to know was just how deep Blakely's ties were to the O'Sullivan family. Because from the sound of things, she knew the man pretty well.

O'Sullivan was definitely connected enough to pull off the kind of theft and cover-up that had landed Gray in jail. Especially with the help of an inside man.

Or woman. And twenty million was a big incentive. Especially with a ready-made scapegoat.

Gray folded his arms over his chest, sizing up the officers in front of him. He could continue to block their path, but there wasn't value in doing it. Not only would it not prevent Martin from being arrested and taken in, but it could also potentially land Gray's butt back behind bars.

Nope, not worth it.

However, there might be information to gain and some goodwill to bank. Without glancing behind him, Gray raised his voice and said, "Martin, are you going to leave peacefully with the nice gentlemen waiting to take you downtown?"

"Yes."

Cocking an eyebrow, Gray held up a single finger to ask for a moment, then turned his back to the officers so he could face Blakely and her father.

Gray's gaze skipped across her, as he tried to find a clue that might help him determine something about the state of her mind. But all he could see was a jumbled mess of fear, irritation and determination.

That didn't tell him much, other than that she was a good daughter who loved her father.

"Martin, I'm going to follow the officers and meet you at the station. Take some unsolicited advice and keep your mouth shut until the lawyer I'm about to call gets there."

Blakely made a strangled sound before she opened her mouth to say something. Gray held up a hand, silencing her before she could get out a single word.

Both she and Whittaker shut their mouths. Gray waved behind him for the officers to come forward and then moved out of the way. He didn't bother to watch the commotion in front of him as they cuffed her father. Instead, he watched Blakely.

And because he did, he was probably the only one who noticed the way her body flinched at the sound of the cuffs snapping together around his wrists. Her mouth thinned with unhappiness at the same time her teeth chewed at the inside of her cheek.

Gray didn't even think she was aware that she was doing it.

She started to take a step to follow the officers as they led away her father, but one of them called out behind him, "Stay where you are, ma'am."

Everyone waited and watched. The sound of people shuffling uncomfortably where they stood was like the unsettling scratching of leaves against a window in the middle of the night.

Once Martin was out of view, in unison, all of the spectators turned toward Blakely. And that's when her face flamed bright red.

But Gray had to hand it to her—she didn't bow under the weight of the embarrassment or scrutiny. Instead, she let her gaze travel slowly around the hallway, as she looked each and every person square in the eye. She practically dared them to ask a question or make a snide remark.

No one did.

Dammit, he didn't want to be impressed with her backbone.

Walking up beside her, Gray grasped her arm. She tensed and he could feel her about to jerk away from him.

Pressing close, he murmured low enough so only she could hear, "You probably don't want to make an even bigger scene."

The sound of her breath dragging deep into her lungs shouldn't have had any effect on him. Neither should the way her body brushed against his with the motion. And yet, it did.

"Do you really think I care about making a scene?" she whispered back.

"Yes, I do."

He was close enough to hear her teeth grinding together. But she didn't refute his statement. Because they both knew it was true.

"Now, be a good girl—walk quietly down the hall with me and I'll take you to your father."

A low, growling, frustrated sound rolled through her. "I really don't like you."

Gray laughed, the sound filling the space between them. "Sweetheart, the feeling is mutual."

Propelling her down the hallway in front of him, Gray chose to ignore the pointed expression on Stone's face as they walked past him. No doubt, he was going to hear about this the next time he and his friend were alone.

So Gray would simply avoid Stone for a little while.

Gray and Blakely were both silent as they headed out of the building and into the parking garage.

Blakely took the first opportunity to speed up and break the hold he had on her. Which was fine with him. And, no, he didn't flex his hand because it was tingling where he'd touched her bare skin.

Several paces ahead of him, it was clear Blakely intended to take her own car. He could have redirected her, but decided to wait and see how long it took her to realize she didn't have her purse or keys.

She was halfway there when she came to a sudden halt. Her head dropped back and he didn't need a clear view in order to know she was squeezing her eyes shut and probably asking a higher power for strength.

Not that she needed any. For all her faults, Blakely Whittaker was one of the strongest women he'd ever met. Not that he was going to tell her that.

It only took her a few seconds to gather herself, turn and head back toward the entrance to the building.

"Don't bother. I'll take you."

"No, thank you." Her words were formal, but there was no real appreciation behind them. Not that he particularly cared. He wasn't letting her drive. Not because he was worried about her state of mind—or not just because. He wanted to make damn sure he was a fly on the wall.

"Look, you can waste precious time going back inside or you can ride with me to the station. Either way, I'm heading there, and if you don't come with me, I'm going to get there first. And something tells me you'd prefer me not to speak to your father without you."

"Why are you doing this?"

"Doing what? Being nice?"

"No, being a pain in my ass."

"I didn't realize helping your father could be viewed as being a pain in your ass."

Blakely's eyes narrowed. A string of expletives flowed from her lips, some of which were quite inventive. He was impressed and, considering he was a convicted felon and had heard a whole hell of a lot, that wasn't an easy feat.

Stalking past him, Blakely headed straight for his car, parked a few spaces from the door. It didn't escape his notice that she knew exactly which one was his. Intelligence gathering or something more?

Standing beside the passenger door, she glared at him over the hood. The tap of her foot against concrete rang out, a perfect staccato of irritation and impatience.

If there wasn't a reason to hurry, Gray would have slowed down on principle alone. And because he knew it would bother her. But he wanted to reach her father as quickly as she did. Maybe more.

The drive to the station was silent, the air between them thick with tension and the familiar scent of her perfume. Sweet and exotic. Floral, yet somehow spicy. It had been tempting him for days. The office they were using wasn't exactly small, but when that scent filled the space...

The front seat of his Bugatti was even worse. Normally, it was his sanctuary. The car was the one frivolous, flashy and over-the-top thing he'd allowed himself once he was out of prison. Today, with Blakely so close beside him, it felt just as much like a prison as the cell he'd been assigned.

He couldn't help but wonder if her scent would be stronger if he buried his face between her thighs?

Gray willed away his response. Nope, he wasn't going there.

He might not be naive enough to believe he had to actually like someone in order to be physically attracted to them. But he *was* smart enough to realize his situation with Blakely was complicated enough without adding mindless sex. And that's all that could be between them.

The fifteen-minute drive felt like an eternity. As soon as he pulled into a space in front of the station, Blakely shot from the car. She was halfway across the lot before he'd even turned off the ignition.

Not that her haste would make much difference. She wasn't going to get very far with the officers inside.

Tucking his hands into his pockets, Gray strolled leisurely after her. Once he entered the station he could hear her voice, already raised in frustration.

"I just need to speak to him for a minute. That's all."

"Ma'am, your father is being processed. You can't see him right now."

Gray bypassed the commotion, choosing to approach another officer at the far end of the counter who was protected by a half wall of bulletproof glass.

"Excuse me," he said. "I'm Gray Lockwood, here

to see my client, Martin Whittaker. He's just been brought in."

The desk sergeant barely glanced up from a stack of papers. "Are you his attorney?"

"Yes."

He shuffled a few more things. "I'll let them know you're here. Take a seat. Someone'll get you in a few."

"Excellent."

Gray gave the man a polite smile, even though he wouldn't notice it, and turned to sit in one of the chairs lining the far wall. They were hard plastic—no doubt, the cheapest thing the city could buy. The metal legs had been scratched to hell and back. Clearly a lot of people had spent time waiting in them over the years.

With a huff, Blakely collapsed into the chair beside him.

"They won't let me see him."

"Really? How surprising."

Blakely gave him a grimace, her only response to his obvious sarcasm.

"Why did we come here if we weren't planning to see him?"

"I have no idea why you decided to follow your father. And I have every intention of seeing him."

"You do?"

"Yes."

"Oh."

Gray knew exactly what wrong conclusion Blakely had just jumped to. And he had no intention of disabusing her of the notion. At least not until it suited his purposes.

Several minutes ticked by. There was motion and activity all around them, but Gray was content to wait. He'd done a lot of that in his adult life. And he'd learned quickly it was a waste of energy to wish things were different. He'd gotten very good at accepting situations as they were, not as he'd prefer them to be. It saved heartache and disappointment.

Blakely, however, was a bucket of nerves and energy. She couldn't settle and constantly shifted in her seat. Crossed and uncrossed her legs. Cracked her knuckles.

Unable to take any more, Gray reached out and placed a hand on her knee. Blakely immediately stilled. In fact, she stopped moving entirely, not even taking a breath.

Her heat seeped into his skin, making his entire arm hum with unexpected energy.

Shit.

"Mr. Lockwood, please follow me."

Thank God for small favors. Gray looked up at the officer standing at the far doorway. He pushed up from the chair and was halfway across the room before he realized Blakely was following him.

This was gonna be good.

Gray gave the officer a polite smile as he walked past.

"Ma'am, I'm sorry, you're not allowed back here."

Pausing in the hallway, he turned in time to catch Blakely's pointed gesture. "I'm with him."

"Are you part of Mr. Whittaker's legal team?"

"No, I'm his daughter."

The officer shook his head. "I'm sorry. Mr. Whittaker is being questioned. Only legal counsel is allowed into the room."

"Then why is he going back?"

"Mr. Lockwood? Because he's acting counsel."

Blakely stared at him, her gaze narrowing. Gray shrugged. "I mentioned that I have a law degree."

"You don't practice."

"No, I'm fortunate enough that I only take the cases I want to. I'm taking your father's." At least for the moment. Gray had every intention of calling in a few favors to get someone else to actually take Martin's case. While he could do it himself, he had other concerns at the moment and didn't need the distraction.

However, he was going to take this prime opportunity to learn everything he could from Martin about Blakely and her connections to the O'Sullivan family. And whether that could have played into how Gray had found himself framed for embezzlement.

"Tell him I'm with you," Blakely demanded, pointing at the officer standing between them.

"Ah, but you're not."

Four

Blakely wanted to scream. Or find something hard to throw straight at his head. Probably not smart, considering there were at least half a dozen people standing close who could arrest her for assault.

Gray Lockwood was as frustrating as he was sexy. That knowing smirk twisting his gorgeous lips… How could she want to kiss the hell out of him at the same time she wanted to shake him?

What was wrong with her?

Blakely watched him disappear down the hallway, irritation churning in her belly. Dropping back into a hard chair, she stared at the door. And waited.

Conspiracy to commit murder.

God, how could this get any worse? Her father was about to go to jail for a very long time. Sure, he'd been in and out her entire life, but for small crimes. Ten months here, two years there. This would be different.

She wanted to believe him when he said he wasn't guilty…but she just couldn't kill that last spark of doubt taunting her from the back of her brain. Her father had a habit of bending the truth.

And Gray… She didn't trust him further than she could throw him. Like every other criminal she'd ever met—and plenty had marched through her life—they all insisted they were innocent.

She'd yet to meet one who actually was. Especially her father.

But a bigger part of her just couldn't believe he could be responsible for anything close to murder. Her father might be a con man and a thief, but he'd never been violent. Hell, he didn't even own a gun.

Gray, on the other hand, was dangerous as hell. Only he didn't need a gun to be that way. The hum in her blood proved that point nicely. She didn't even like him, but he had the ability to make her body react.

Blakely didn't need the details to know he'd been through a lot. The scar through his eyebrow and the rock-hard muscles he now sported hadn't been earned by doing bench presses and back squats. But there was more to him than his physically intimidating presence. He was quiet and observant. Gray saw too much.

She'd watched him over the last several days, not just as he interacted with her, but with others at the office. He watched and cataloged. Almost as if he was gathering intel on everyone who moved through his existence, even if they only touched his life in the most minor way.

He hadn't been that way when she'd known him before.

Clearly, he brought value to Stone Surveillance. On several occasions Stone and Finn had come to consult Gray's opinion on a case they were working.

She didn't want to see anything good in him. She didn't want to believe he was helping her father. She wanted to see him only as the criminal he was. Without that concerning history, it would be so much more difficult to keep her distance. To pretend she hadn't noticed the layer of humanity and honor. She definitely didn't want to like him. Because right now, she was having a damn hard time keeping her awareness of him in check.

Lucky for her, watching him walk through that precinct door without her was just the reminder she needed.

When she saw him again, he was going to get an earful.

Selfish bastard.

Gray walked into the room and immediately flashbacks assaulted him. A shiver of apprehension raced down his spine, but he refused to let it take hold.

He wasn't the one being questioned here.

Although, being in the small, nondescript, uncomfortable room made it difficult not to let bad memories take over. The barrage of questions he hadn't understood or known the answers to. Feeling blindsided and out of his element. Cut loose without a safety net.

Those first few hours of being questioned had been disorienting because he didn't have a clue what any of the investigators were talking about. And since he'd been innocent, he'd waived his right to counsel. His first mistake.

The detective sitting across the table from Martin glanced up as he entered the room, but didn't say anything. Martin's eyes skipped distractedly over Gray, a puzzled expression filling his face. "Why are you here?"

Gray's first impressions of Martin weren't great. He was the complete opposite of Blakely—scattered, loud and obnoxious. Or at least he had been so far. Although, he also appeared to know exactly who Gray was, which wasn't surprising considering the role Blakely had played in the well-publicized, high-profile trial that had completely turned Gray's life upside down.

"I'm part of your legal team—why wouldn't I be here?"

Martin quirked an eyebrow, but he didn't vocalize the obvious question. Smart man, considering a detective was sitting across from him.

Gray turned to the officer. "I'd like a few minutes with my client, please." The statement might have technically been a request…but it really wasn't.

A frown crunched the corners of the detective's weathered and weary eyes. He stood without saying a word and the door squeaked shut behind him as he left.

Martin opened his mouth, but before he could say anything Gray shook his head. He assumed they were being recorded and watched, and intended to act accordingly.

Taking the vacated chair, Gray folded his hands on the table between them.

"The rest of your legal team should be arriving shortly."

"Why are you doing this?"

An expected question for sure, but one Gray wasn't prepared to answer. At least not here. And not entirely honestly.

"Blakely works for my company and we take care of our own."

Martin scoffed. "Blakely might think I'm gullible, and maybe occasionally I am, but I wasn't born yesterday, son."

Maybe not, but something told him Martin Whittaker wasn't entirely smart when it came to the world, either. Or that was the impression Gray had gotten from Blakely. And he might not trust her, but she was smart as hell and rather aware of what was going on around her.

"Let's just say I have a vested interest in keeping your daughter focused on a project she's working on with me. I won't have her full attention if she's concerned about you. Money isn't important to me, but right now her assistance is. Buying peace of mind by providing your legal team is a smart strategy for me to get what I want."

Martin slowly nodded. "You could have easily accomplished that without lying to the officers and coming in here to see me."

"Perhaps, but I don't know you."

"True."

"And had no idea whether you'd be smart about what you said until the lawyers I've retained arrive. Besides, I didn't lie. I have a legal degree and specialize in criminal defense."

"But you're not taking my case."

"No, I don't have the luxury of splitting my focus right now, either."

Martin hummed in the back of his throat. "Still doesn't explain why you came all the way down here."

He might be gullible, but Martin Whittaker clearly had enough street smarts to go with his naivete.

"I have a couple questions for you."

"About the charges against me?"

"No."

Martin tugged at the cuffs wrapped around his wrists, rattling the chain connected to the ring bolted to the table. The movement had been instinctive, a gesture he couldn't quite complete.

"Then what?"

"Tell me about your relationship with O'Sullivan. How long have you known him?"

Martin's head tipped sideways as he considered for several seconds before carefully answering. "Ryan and I grew up in the same neighborhood. I've known him for the better part of fifty years."

Interesting. Gray was surprised he'd never heard Martin's name before, all things considered. "And how well does Blakely know him?"

"Not very well." Martin's answer was a little too quick and adamant for Gray's taste.

Perhaps he'd asked the wrong question. "How well does Ryan know Blakely?"

Martin gave him a knowing smile that made Gray wonder whether his scattered persona was all an act.

"Ryan's been in Blakely's life since her birth. Although, my daughter would prefer that not to be the case. He's her godfather and helped put her through college."

Right. Gray stared at the other man, wondering just how to use the information he'd been given to find out if Ryan and Martin had used Blakely's connections at Lockwood Industries in order to steal twenty million dollars and frame Gray. Martin wasn't likely to admit it, especially in the middle of a police station.

And asking outright would tip his hand. Better to have Joker do some digging. The problem they'd run into before was having no real direction to start looking.

Gray began to push up from his chair, but the next words out of Martin's mouth stalled him halfway up.

"My daughter, however, is completely unaware and she'd never speak to me again if she found out Ryan paid for her education. My daughter is proud and honorable to a fault."

While most fathers would say those words with pride in their voices, Martin's tone conveyed disappointment. Gray had to shake his head.

"If Ryan was on fire, Blakely wouldn't cross the street to spit on him. She would, however, cross to throw some gasoline."

Well, that was pretty definitive. And left little room for the idea that Blakely would do anything to help Ryan O'Sullivan. Although, if she really had, no doubt her father would be the first to say whatever he could to deflect suspicion.

So this conversation had done rather little to help Gray decide whether Blakely had been involved in framing him, or had just lucked into information that had been planted.

A knock on the door prevented him from asking any more questions, even if he'd had any.

The detective stood in the open doorway, a very pissed off Blakely glaring from behind him.

Blakely stormed out of the station. She was halfway to Gray's car when he grasped her arm and jerked her to a stop.

Turning to glare at him, she ripped her arm from his grasp. But instead of turning away again, she leaned forward into his personal space and growled, "Don't touch me."

Her blood whooshed in her veins. The sound of it throbbed through her head, along with the tattoo of her elevated breathing.

Seriously, she needed to get a grip.

Logically, she realized the emotion directed at Gray was not entirely his fault. Everything that had happened today was simply coming to a head, crashing down over her at once. And he made a handy target.

But realizing that didn't do her much good.

Glancing around them, Gray frowned. How was it fair that the man could still manage to look like a Hollywood heartthrob even while irritated?

Ignoring her snarled words, he grasped her arm again and urged her ahead of him and around the corner of the building.

He maneuvered them both into a dark patch of quiet shade. Using his leverage, he set her back against the brick wall and then let her go.

He backed away, putting a few feet between them. "Now isn't the time to lose it, Blakely."

"No joke."

Gray cocked a single eyebrow, silently calling her ten kinds of stupid for doing exactly what she shouldn't be doing.

It stung that he was right. Blakely groaned. Dropping her head back, she let her body sag into the rough surface of the wall. The sharp edges scraped against her skin, but she didn't care.

"I'm pissed at you. I'm pissed at him. I'm just—"

"Pissed. Yeah, I got that."

"He promised me. And I'm such an idiot for believing him because it's not like he hasn't broken a million promises before. But I couldn't stop myself from hoping, even when I knew I shouldn't."

God, she knew better. But it was so difficult to cut those ties. And that's what it would take in order for her to be free of her father's drama and messes. The only way to avoid it all would be to avoid him. And she wasn't to that point yet.

Or she hadn't been.

Her mother and sister had given up on him years ago.

"Perhaps he's being honest and really is innocent."

Blakely stared at Gray, the echo of his words slightly eerie, all things considered. Was he saying that because no one—including her—had believed *him* when he said he was innocent? Was he being just as naive as she was?

"I've heard that before, Gray." And, no, she wasn't just talking about her father.

"Well, I believe him. I've called in a few favors and arranged for a friend to represent him."

"Why would you do that?"

"Funny, he asked me the same question. And I'll give you the same answer. Because I need you fully focused on helping me prove my innocence, and you won't be as long as you're worried about him. I have the money and connections to afford the best representation for Martin."

Blakely shook her head. "No, I won't let you do that. We don't need your money or your help."

The statement, vehement though she tried to make it sound, was a complete lie. She did need his help. And his money, in the form of the salary he was paying her to help him on this wild-goose chase.

"We don't want your charity."

"Too bad, you're getting it, anyway."

"I refuse to accept your help, Gray." There was one sure way she knew to get him angry enough to back down and agree to leave her and her father alone. "You're a criminal, just like Ryan. I won't go to him for help and I won't accept it from you."

Gray's expression went stone-hard. His mouth thinned and his eyes glittered a warning it was too late to heed.

He took a measured step, closing the gap between them. Blakely swallowed even as a frisson of awareness snaked down her spine. Nope, she refused to give in to it.

He shifted. The soft brush of his body against hers made her skin flush hot and a molten center of need melt deep inside her. His voice was low and measured as he leaned close and murmured, "I'm nothing like Ryan O'Sullivan, although you already know that. Don't get me wrong—I'm ten times as dangerous as he is, only because I have very little left to lose. The difference is I have standards and morals."

The heat of his breath tickled her skin. His lips were so close and she wanted them on her.

No, she didn't.

Blakely tipped her head backward. She tried to crowd into the wall, but there was nowhere for her to go. Nowhere to get away from him. Or get away from her own unwanted reaction.

This close, all she could see were his eyes. His expression. The desolation and hope. The pain and the heat. The intensity centered squarely on her.

The spot at the juncture of her thighs throbbed. The breath in her lungs caught as the warmth of his body invaded every pore of her skin.

Gray Lockwood *was* dangerous. To her sanity. Her peace of mind. The very foundation of her personal morals. She'd spent her entire life avoiding men like him. And she wasn't just talking about his criminal past, although that surely should have been enough to give her pause.

But it was more.

Gray Lockwood was a force to be reckoned with. He was intelligent, observant, dynamic and demanding. In his youth, that combination had manifested in an entitled attitude that had been less than attractive.

Now, those same qualities had the ability to make her panties damp. She shouldn't be turned on by his confidence and domineering attitude. But she was.

Blakely stared up at him, her lips parted. Waiting. Although for what, she wasn't entirely certain.

Gray seemed poised, as well—on the edge of something neither of them wanted to want, but couldn't stop. So close to her, Blakely could feel the tension coiled in every one of his muscles. He was like a tiger, waiting to spring.

The moment stretched between them. On the far side of the building, a police siren went off. A couple exited the building and chatted, although Blakely couldn't have said what their conversation was about.

She breathed in, filling her lungs with the tantalizing scent that had been taunting her for days. Him.

"To hell with it," he finally murmured right before his body pressed in against her.

All the air whooshed out of her lungs, as if he'd slammed her against the wall, although he hadn't. Excitement flashed through her as his mouth dropped to hers.

Blakely's gasp backed into her lungs as he kissed her, swallowing the sound.

Gray's arm snaked around her, settling on the small of her back as he pulled her closer. His other hand found her face, cupping it and angling her just where he wanted.

The first touch was light, but that didn't last long. Seconds later, Gray was opening his lips, diving in and demanding everything from her.

His tongue tangled with hers, stroking and stoking and driving the need she'd been ignoring into a raging inferno she couldn't deny. Seconds—that's how long it took for him to steal her resolve and leave her a shaking mess of desire.

Her own hands gripped his shoulders, pulling him closer even as her brain screamed that she needed to push him away.

But she couldn't make herself do it.

The angle changed. The kiss deepened. He demanded more. And Blakely didn't hesitate to give it. Going up on her toes, she met him force for force. Need for need.

Somehow her leg raised, hooking up over his hip

as she made demands of her own. The overheated center of her sex ached. Blakely moaned in the back of her throat as she undulated against him, looking for relief.

The sound seemed to snap him out of whatever had tangled them together.

Hands gripping her arms, he pushed away, unraveling their intertwined bodies. She leaned into his hold, unconsciously pushing against the invisible barrier he'd placed between them.

"I'm sorry," he said.

"I'm not." Blakely wanted to slap a hand across her wayward mouth, but it was too late. This was his fault. He'd obviously fried her brain.

Shaking his head, Gray gave a soft chuckle. "Thanks for being honest. But I shouldn't have done that."

Blakely wasn't going to argue with him. "You're right."

She expected Gray to walk away, leave her there and let her figure out her own way back to the office.

Instead, he reached out, soft fingers trailing lightly over her cheek. "I've wanted to do that for days." His heated gaze skipped across the features of her face, following his teasing fingertip.

His honesty unnerved her, although it also settled her. It was reassuring to know she wasn't the only one fighting against urges she shouldn't have.

But she also couldn't pretend. "This can't happen." Blakely tried to make the words sound adamant, even if a huge part of her didn't want them to be.

Gray nodded, but his words contradicted the action. "Why not? We're both adults."

"Yes, but you don't like me and I don't like you."

Gray's eyes jumped back to hers, staring straight into her. "That's not true. I like you just fine."

Blakely couldn't stop the scoffing sound that scraped through her throat. "Yeah, right. You hate me. I was instrumental in putting you in jail."

"Maybe."

There was no *maybe* about it. Her testimony had been key to his conviction.

"I'm attracted to you, Blakely. We're working closely together, which makes ignoring the physical pull difficult. You tell me you're not interested and I'll do just that. But knowing you are…"

Blakely understood completely. Her body still hummed with the memory of their kiss. "It's going to be hell to put that genie back in the bottle."

Five

It had been two days since the kiss. Since he'd grabbed her, pressed her against the wall and gotten the first intoxicating taste of her mouth.

Nope, the feel of her hadn't been haunting him.

Gray sat on the opposite side of the room from her, trying to concentrate on a stack of evidence, just as he had for the last two days. Honestly, if Stone walked in right now and asked him what he was doing, Gray couldn't have told him. He hadn't actually absorbed anything he'd read for hours.

This wasn't good. Or productive.

For her part, Blakely had chosen to pretend the kiss never happened. When they'd walked away from the police station, Gray hadn't been entirely certain what her reaction would be. The fact that she hadn't slapped him was promising. And there was no way she could deny being just as into that kiss as he'd been.

But by the next morning, her stiff, perfect facade had been back in place.

Honestly, he preferred Blakely when she was energetic and emotional. Real and authentic. He'd seen the evidence that she could be more than just a disapproving robot who followed all the rules because she was scared of what might happen if she didn't.

His conversation with Martin had been rather enlightening, though. Discovering Blakely had grown up on the outskirts of a major crime family shed some light, for sure.

But after his little meeting at the police station, one thing had become crystal clear—neither Blakely nor Martin were sitting on twenty million dollars. First, if they had been, Blakely wouldn't have been worried about paying for her father's lawyer. She would have called up the best defense attorney money could buy. Second, if they had that kind of money, neither of them would still be in Charleston.

Gray was convinced Martin might act the fool, but was far from it. He used that facade to his advantage. But the man wouldn't stick around near the scene of the crime if he had the means to disappear and live the good life.

While that didn't precisely mean Blakely hadn't been inadvertently involved in the frame job that had sent Gray to prison, it did, at least in his mind, clear her of intentionally setting him up.

Blakely had been just as much a pawn in the whole scheme as he'd been. It was possible that whoever had placed the trail of financial information in the Lockwood Industries books had simply banked on *someone* finding the crumbs.

It really wouldn't have mattered who that someone was. In fact, it might have played better if the someone was completely innocent and unconnected. If the police had done a thorough job—which Gray wasn't willing to concede—they should have investigated every witness just to be certain of their character before they took the stand.

Squeezing his eyes shut, Gray shoved away the file he'd been looking at and dropped back into his chair.

He and Blakely had been pouring over testimony, evidence and notes for a week. And so far, they'd found absolutely nothing.

The only thing Gray had to show for his effort was a growing certainty that Blakely had been unwittingly involved. Which benefited him not at all. It would have been easier if she had been purposely involved. Because then he wouldn't have felt guilty for the way he'd maneuvered her into helping him.

Or for the way he wanted to cross the room, pull her out of her chair, wipe everything off the desk and kiss every inch of her naked skin.

Opening his eyes, Gray glanced across the office. It probably wasn't smart to have his desk facing Blakely's if he wanted to ignore the awareness pulsing beneath the surface of his skin.

Not that it really mattered. He didn't need to be

watching her to know she was there. Gray could feel her presence the minute she walked into the room.

Right now, though, it made his lips pull down at the edges to watch her. Because bent over a file spread open on her desk, one hand lodged in her hair and her forehead crinkled with a frown, she looked just as frustrated and unhappy as he was.

And despite everything, he didn't want her to feel that way.

"Let's get out of here." The words were out of his mouth before he even realized he'd meant to say them.

"What?" Blakely looked up at him, blinking owlishly. Her entire body stayed poised over the file, which only made him want to take her away from here even more. It took several seconds for her gaze to clear and focus on him.

"Let's get out of here."

Her head tilted to the side. He was starting to learn she did that when she was weighing things. What she should do against what she wanted to do. Or what everyone else expected of her against what her instincts told her.

He was tired of seeing her calculate every step before taking one. Sure, there was a time in his life when he didn't calculate anything because he knew there were a pile of safety nets—not to mention billions of dollars—to save him if he fell flat on his face.

Trust him to land in a mess that would rip the safety nets out from under him and make his billions worthless in getting him out of the jam.

However, that didn't mean Blakely's approach

to life was any better. If there was one thing he'd learned, it was that life was short. You never knew what was going to happen or where you were going to end up. It was your responsibility to make the most of where you were while you were there.

He had a feeling Blakely rarely allowed herself that pleasure.

Gray also knew that if he gave her enough time to come up with a valid excuse, she'd decline his offer simply because he made her nervous. Not because she was scared of him, but because she didn't want to like him.

Or want him.

Well, that wasn't going to work for him anymore.

He wanted her and he wasn't going to let the mess they were trying to unravel stop him from getting what he wanted.

Standing up, Gray walked around to her desk. "Let's go."

"Go where?"

"Does it matter? We both need a break. I haven't seen you eat anything today. You've got to be starving."

She paused. Gray's stomach knotted with nerves that he really didn't want to acknowledge or investigate. And to his surprise, Blakely offered him a small half smile.

"I am pretty hungry."

What the hell was she doing?

For the second time in a few days, Blakely found

herself riding in the passenger seat of Gray's low-slung sports car. The leather cupped her body, making her feel snug and safe even as he tore through the city at breakneck speed. Apparently, he wasn't concerned about getting the attention of an officer... or a speeding ticket.

She should have said no and stayed at the office. Not just because avoiding small, enclosed spaces with Gray was just smart. But because she was seriously starting to think the man was innocent of the charges for which he'd been convicted.

And that left her with a nasty taste in her mouth.

They'd spent a lot of time together in the last week. In that time, one thing had become obvious. The man he was now was nowhere near the man he'd been back then.

And, yes, that did nothing to prove he'd been innocent. Gray's reputation back then might have been difficult to surmount. But, honestly, had he really been that terrible?

No. He'd been an entitled prick who'd had everything handed to him on a silver platter, but even as he'd partied and gambled and gone jet-setting around the world, he'd been generous to a fault.

Blakely had also discovered that while he'd been blowing millions on random and pointless things, he'd also established a foundation to assist underprivileged children with college scholarships. He'd been involved in a local fine-arts program, paying to keep art and music in schools that no longer had funding. He'd donated millions to drug-rehabilitation programs and randomly provided money to just about every charitable organization that approached him for a donation.

The information had been brought up in court, which was how she'd discovered the truth. But the prosecutor had implied it was easy to write a check, especially when one needed the tax write-off.

Blakely couldn't dispute that, but something told her the donations had been more than some accountant telling him it was a good money move. The amount he'd donated in the three years leading up to the embezzlement had been significant. In fact, it had been almost half of what he'd been accused of stealing.

Which made no sense. Why would he steal money only to donate it?

He wouldn't. Which had been his argument all along. He didn't need the twenty million. The prosecution had argued need wasn't the only motivation to explain his actions. But Gray hardly struck her as the kind of person who would steal simply to prove he could.

The attorneys also detailed a contentious relationship with his father. Several Lockwood employees testified to arguments and tension between the two in the office. Gray's father was fed up with his irresponsible ways and wanted him to take on more responsibility within the company. Their implied motive for the theft was revenge against his father, but Blakely couldn't see how stealing twenty million from Lockwood had harmed Gray's father. Certainly, the company had struggled for several months, but they'd pulled through just fine.

It all circled back to the fact that Gray hardly needed the money. Which was honestly how she found herself sitting in the seat beside him.

She was starting to like him. Starting to realize the man she'd forced into a round hole was really more complicated than she'd given him credit for.

She'd misjudged him, then and now.

The question was, what was she going to do about it?

"Where are we going?" Blakely finally asked, filling the charged silence stretching between them.

"A little place I know."

That really didn't answer her question. "Where?"

Gray swiveled his head, studying her instead of the road for several seconds. Normally, especially at this speed, that would have made her nervous, but she had no doubt Gray had complete control of his car.

"Do you trust me?"

What a loaded question. Did she? No, but then she didn't really trust anyone. And while she was beginning to think she'd misjudged Gray, that didn't mean she was ready to place her life in his hands.

However, that wasn't necessarily what he was asking.

"To pick a good place to get food? Yes."

Gray's mouth tipped up into a lopsided, knowing grin. He understood precisely what she was saying.

"Excellent. We gotta start somewhere."

Did they?

Blakely's stomach flipped at the idea. She wanted to, that was clear. Even sitting this close to him was doing crazy and unexplainable things to her body. Her skin tingled and heat settled deep in her belly. Her panties were damp and he hadn't even touched her.

He drove her out to a little place near Rainbow Row. It was quaint and small, not exactly what she'd expected him to pick. But even more surprising, she hadn't heard of it.

"I've never been here," she said, staring up at the front as she climbed from the car. Better that than stare at him as he held open her door. Or get tangled up in thinking how easy it would be to lean into the hard planes of his body, press her lips to his and drown in another mind-bending kiss.

Was it her imagination, or did he linger a little longer than necessary before moving out of her way?

"I'm not surprised. It's fairly new, but the food is amazing."

"I guess I'll find out."

It was past the normal lunch rush, but there were still a handful of occupied tables. Mostly older women with their makeup and hair done, obviously out for lunch with friends. There were several affluent neighborhoods close by, so not altogether surprising.

The hostess was pleasant and nice, even if she did stare at Gray a little longer than necessary. But who could blame her? Take away the criminal element and the man was a walking fantasy. Polished, but still with the hint of a few rough edges. He carried himself with a confidence that was both attractive and enviable.

But Blakely wouldn't allow herself to be jealous. Mostly because she had nothing to be jealous about.

The perky hostess showed them to a table in the far corner, beside a window that overlooked a lush garden. The empty tables surrounding them created an illusion of privacy, which might not be a good thing.

Gray held out her chair, brushing his fingers over the curve of her shoulders as he pulled away. All this time, Blakely had assumed holding chairs was simply a polite thing for men to do. Now she realized it was a perfect excuse. That simple touch had sent a low hum vibrating through her body and she was going to spend the next hour fighting to turn it off.

How could she manufacture a reason for him to touch her again?

Nope, she wasn't going there. Picking up the menu, Blakely studied it rather than Gray. After a few moments, the words actually started to make sense.

Their waitress was friendly, and she obviously knew Gray, judging by their conversation. But she was also efficient, as she took their drink orders and highlighted the day's specials. Blakely ordered a pecan-crusted chicken salad that sounded amazing. Gray ordered pimento cheese and homemade pork rinds, followed by pan-seared tuna and asparagus.

Once the menus were taken and some soft rolls appeared on the table, there was nothing left to keep her distracted. Which wasn't necessarily a good thing.

For the first time, Blakely realized Gray had positioned her in a chair with her back to the rest of the room...filling the spot right in front of her with nothing but him. Sneaky man. Had he done that on purpose?

Blakely was trying to decide whether to ask him—because maybe she really didn't want the answer—when Gray's cell, sitting facedown on the table, buzzed. Frowning, he flipped it over. The frown went from a mild crease to full-blown irritation as soon as he read whatever was on the screen. Glancing up, he said, "I'm sorry, I need to get this."

Blakely waved away his apology. They weren't on a date so he didn't need to justify his actions to her.

She expected him to get up and walk away, to gain a little bit of privacy. Instead, he just answered the call, so she could hear his side of the conversation.

"Hello, Mother."

If Blakely hadn't been able to see Gray's expression, the tone in his voice would have clearly conveyed his displeasure. She wondered if that was his normal reaction to his mother, or if there was something specific going on between them. Not that it was any of her business.

Hell, she could identify. It wasn't like she rejoiced whenever her father's name popped up on her cell screen. He never called her when things were going well.

"Calm down." Gray's eyes narrowed, the irritation quickly morphing to something more. "I have no idea what you're talking about." He paused, listening to something on the other end before letting out a sigh. "I'll be there in a few minutes."

Hanging up, he dropped his phone onto the table

with a loud clatter that made her concerned for the safety of the screen. "I'm sorry to cut this short, but I need to run over to my mother's house."

"So I gathered."

Waving over their waitress, Gray didn't bother asking for the check. He slipped a hundred into her hand and then stood, holding out an arm for Blakely to go in front of him.

The walk to the car was silent, mostly because she didn't know what to say.

What she didn't expect, once they got inside, was for Gray to head in the opposite direction of the office.

Apparently, she was about to meet his mother.

Six

Gray wasn't looking forward to this confrontation at all. And part of him felt like an ass for dragging Blakely along for the ride. But his mother had been spouting an irate tirade of nonsense and he was afraid to take the time to drop off Blakely at the office, which was in the opposite direction.

With any luck, he could calm his mother and they could be back to work in less than half an hour.

Although, he wasn't holding his breath.

It had been just about eleven months since he'd last spoken to or seen his mother. Before that, it had been seven years. He'd stopped by the estate after getting out of prison. Although he hadn't exactly expected the fatted calf to be slaughtered, an acknowledgment of his place in her life would have been nice.

Instead, she'd followed his father's line and refused to even let him inside the front door.

Who knew if she'd let him inside this time, either. Not that he particularly cared. His mother hadn't exactly been a warm and loving example of motherhood to begin with. The minute his father disowned him she'd taken that as permission to pretend he didn't exist.

There was a spiteful, vindictive part of him that enjoyed knowing her friends talked about her behind her back because of him. If nothing else, being wrongly convicted of a crime gave him that perk. Although, it hardly outweighed the cons.

It took about five minutes to get to the estate on Legare Street from the restaurant. Not nearly long enough.

He climbed out of the car and headed for the front door. Blakely slowly followed. He purposely hadn't asked her to either stay behind or come with him, instead leaving it as her decision.

He figured, after meeting Martin, she could most likely handle his mother in one of her states, anyway.

Gray didn't bother knocking. Why would he, when the estate had been his childhood home? But it did feel weird walking through the front door after such a long time away. The place looked exactly the same—not a single mirror or piece of artwork on the wall had been changed in almost eight years.

Not surprising, either. His mother was a creature of habit. When given an option, she'd take the path of least resistance every time. One reason she'd made such a perfect trophy wife.

After striding down the hallway, Gray bounded up the wide, sweeping staircase to the second floor and the rooms his mother had claimed as her own long ago. Opening the door to the sunroom, he wasn't surprised to see her pacing furiously back and forth.

She didn't turn when he opened the door, apparently so deep in her own discourse that she hadn't heard him enter. But the minute she spotted him, he became the object of her obvious rage.

Charging across the room, she yelled, "Who does this bitch think she is? Blackmailing me after all these years? I had nothing to do with this, dammit! Nothing. And I'm not paying her a single dollar, let alone twenty million."

Gray shook his head, trying to make sense of his mother's words.

But her rant didn't end there. The words continued to come, punctuated by her slamming fists hitting into his chest and rocking him back on his heels.

Well, that was unexpected.

And so was the way Blakely shot between them, shoving into his mother's face and pushing her backward. "What do you think you're doing?"

"I don't know who the hell you are, but get out of my way."

"Not on your life. Whatever's going on, it doesn't give you to the right to physically assault your son."

His mother laughed, the bitter sound of it sending a shiver down his spine.

"He isn't my son."

"Excuse me?" It was Blakely's turn to be knocked backward. She collided with his chest.

Distractedly, Gray wrapped an arm around her waist, holding her tight against him.

His mother's words startled him, but Gray locked down his reaction and refused to show it. This woman had abandoned him long ago and didn't deserve anything from him.

"What the hell do you mean?"

His mother's eyes jerked up to his. The blind fury clouding them slowly faded. "Shit."

Yeah, that pretty much summed up this whole situation.

Waving a hand in the direction of the sofa in front of the floor-to-ceiling windows, she indicated he should sit. Gray didn't bother following her request. But for the first time, he realized she was holding a piece of paper in her hand.

"What's that?"

Frowning, she waved the thing through the air. Just by sight, it appeared to be cheap copy paper. The shadow of several lines of text could be seen through it, so it wasn't very heavy. "This? This would be a blackmail demand."

"Who sent it?"

"You probably should sit."

"I'm good."

"Your father's going to kill me."

"Since he disowned me several years ago, I find it hard to believe he'll care what you say or do."

His mother shook her head, sadness washing over her expression. "That's where you're wrong."

Somehow, he didn't think so. Not only had his father ignored Gray's insistence that he was innocent, but his father had also gone so far as to cut Gray out of his life entirely. What loving parent did that? Gray had always been nothing more than another pawn to the man. Someone his father could control and move at will. And when Gray became a liability instead of an asset, he was sacrificed.

Unlike Stone, whose parents had stood by him, even before they learned the truth—that he'd murdered their friend's son because he'd walked in on an attempted rape. His friend had kept the details to himself for years, protecting the woman he loved. His family had supported him, accepted him. Hell, they'd thrown him a lavish party when he finally got out.

But despite being innocent, *Gray's* family had disowned him, cut him out of the family business and left him alone in the world.

Sure, he could tell himself that he was better off without his mother and father in his life. And, logically, he realized that was absolutely true. But it still hurt like hell when the people who were supposed to have his back had abandoned him.

His mother gave a grimace. "Oh, don't get me wrong. He wouldn't care because *you* know. But he will care that someone else is privy to the dirty laundry he's so desperate to keep hidden."

Now that sounded more like his father. "Well, then,

by all means, tell me. I'd really appreciate having something I could hold over his head."

Especially once Gray had proof of his innocence. Even sweeter to demand access to the company, and also have the means to control the strings on the man who viewed himself as the puppet master.

Blakely, who had taken his mother's suggestion and sat on the sofa several feet away, piped up. "I'm going out on a limb here, but reading between the lines, I'm going to guess that Gray isn't your son, but he is your husband's."

His mother glanced over at Blakely, her gaze moving up and down, taking stock.

What was wrong with him that he wanted his mother to approve of her? Childhood impulses he couldn't control? Wasn't he too old to need parental approval for anything? Especially considering he and his mother hadn't particularly had that kind of relationship to begin with.

Finally, his mother said, "Nailed it in one. She's a smart one."

Yes, she absolutely was. The more time he spent with Blakely, the more he appreciated her quick mind. And he was starting to understand her rock-solid sense of honor, too.

"That note. It's from his biological mother? Demanding money to keep the secret?"

"Pretty much."

"Twenty million. That's what you said earlier?"

"Yes."

Blakely turned her gaze toward him. "Coincidence?"

He knew exactly what she was asking. Was it a coincidence the blackmail demand was the same amount of money that was still missing from the embezzlement? Maybe. It was a nice round figure. Not to mention, the media had been linking that number with his name for years.

But while his release last year had prompted a new flurry of media attention, that had died down in the months since. Partly because both of his friends had taken some of the heat off his back with their own releases and high-profile antics.

But what if it wasn't? They were still looking for that missing twenty million. Maybe his birth mother thought she deserved it? Or maybe she was somehow involved and never got the money she was supposed to get?

"Who is this woman?"

"I don't know."

Yeah, right. That was a lie if ever he'd heard one. His mother might have never gone to college and spent most of her time involved in several charitable organizations coordinating glitzy events, but she was far from ignorant. In fact, she was quite brilliant at gossip and knew exactly how to dig up dirt on just about anyone. There wasn't a snowball's chance in hell she hadn't done—or paid for—a full investigation of her husband's fling. Especially if the woman was the mother of her "child."

He wasn't the only one skeptical. Blakely scoffed. "Please, you don't strike me as stupid."

"Why, thank you, dear." His mother's voice practically dripped syrupy sarcasm all over the floor.

Blakely ignored it. "You know exactly who your son's mother is. You wouldn't be foolish enough to let that important piece of information go until you discovered who it was."

A half smile tugged at his mother's perfect lips. "I like this one. You should keep her around."

"I'll take that under advisement. In the meantime, why don't you answer her question?"

"Fine. I know who she is. Your father wasn't exactly as discreet as he'd like to think."

Gray wasn't entirely certain what to say to that. Sorry? How convenient? So he simply kept his mouth shut and waited.

"She worked at the club. One of those girls that drives a cart around and brings drinks out to the men playing golf. At least, until your father set her up in a nice town house and provided her a monthly stipend to be at his beck and call."

Great, his mother sounded like a winner.

"When she got pregnant, he was pissed. Supposedly, she was on birth control, but the hussy forgot to take it. However, as he always does, your father found a way to make that work in his favor. We'd been trying for years to get pregnant, but couldn't. The doctors weren't hopeful and fertility treatments weren't as advanced back then as they are now. He convinced me that he'd found a woman who'd agreed to a private adoption."

"But you knew."

His mother grimaced. "I knew. I was aware of the affair already. It wasn't the first one and, clearly, wasn't the last. But as long as he was inconspicuous I didn't particularly care."

"You agreed to accept the baby as your own."

With a sigh, his mother walked over to the chair across from Blakely and sat. "I did."

"But you knew," Blakely said. "It wasn't simply that he wasn't yours. It was that he was hers."

His mother looked up at him, regret filling her eyes. "Yes. Every time I looked at you, it was a reminder of your father's infidelity. It was one thing to live with it in the background, but…you look like her."

"I do?"

She nodded. "And him. I tried. I really did, Gray. I wanted you to be my son. And you are."

"But I'm also not."

"It was so hard not to allow you to shoulder the blame for something you had no responsibility for."

Gray nodded. What else could he do? Argue with her? Tell her she should have tried harder? That it wasn't fair for her to agree to accept him as her own, but then not follow through with actually being his mother?

Speaking those truths aloud would change nothing.

"Who is she?"

"Now? She's a showgirl in Vegas. My one requirement was that the adoption be closed and the mother agree to leave the state. Your father paid her a huge sum and she left."

Clearly, his birth mother had been more interested in the money than in her son. And if the letter was any indication, she still was. That was something he'd have to deal with later.

"Do you know how to find her?"

His mother nodded.

"Give me the letter and her information and I'll take care of this."

Reluctantly, his mother handed the letter to him. Without looking, he held it out to Blakely, knowing she'd grab it and keep it safe. When they returned to the office, he'd send it to their forensics team to be analyzed. He'd also contact Joker to see what information he could dig up before heading to Vegas.

Holding out a hand, Gray indicated Blakely should follow him out of the room. She rose, heading in his direction. He stood still, waiting for her to exit first.

And was surprised when her palm landed on his chest and stroked down across his body as she passed. Somehow, that simple touch helped settle the chaos rioting inside him.

He followed her through the house. His mother's footsteps echoed behind his. But before they left, Blakely paused at the front door. Turning, she glanced around him to his mother. "Why did you call Gray instead of your husband?"

"Because Malcolm's indiscretions are the reason we're in this mess in the first place. And I know Gray is part owner of a security firm. I assumed he'd be better equipped to handle the situation than his father."

Blakely nodded. "That's what I thought."

Gray was surprised when she grasped his hand and headed down the wide front steps. Squeezing his hand before she dropped it, Blakely rounded the hood of the car and slid into the passenger seat.

He loved the smooth, graceful way she moved. It was becoming more and more difficult to tear his gaze away from watching her whenever she was close.

Gray slid down into the driver's seat, but before he could put the car in gear, Blakely placed a staying hand over his.

"Are you okay?"

Was he? Gray honestly didn't know. Certainly, his mother's revelation should have rocked his foundation. But it really hadn't. It wasn't like she'd ever been the demonstrative, loving type. Actually, learning he wasn't her real son added context to his childhood. It helped him understand things that had never made sense before.

And he'd actually lost both of his parents long before now, so learning this new detail changed nothing, although it provided another possible motive for what had happened to him.

Which was a good thing.

"Yeah, I'm good."

Blakely stared deep into his eyes. She didn't try and tell him he wasn't okay. She simply searched for clues that he really meant what he'd said.

After several moments, she gave him a sad half

smile and squeezed his hand again. "I'm going with you."

Gray's eyebrows arched up in confusion. "Where?"

"Vegas. Don't pretend you're not going. I'm going with you."

"No, you're not."

"Yes, I am. What would Stone think about you gallivanting off to Vegas by yourself to meet the biological mother you didn't know existed until twenty minutes ago? A woman who may or may not be involved somehow in your embezzlement conviction?"

Oh, she really was good. "That's playing dirty."

Blakely's smile morphed into a megawatt one. "What can I say? I'm learning."

Blakely never expected to find herself sitting across the aisle from Gray on a private plane. Sure, she'd half expected to fly first class for the first time in her life, but this…? Totally unexpected. She was completely out of her element, although tried not to show it.

"Relax."

And she was apparently failing miserably.

"I'm relaxed."

"No, you're not. You're wound tighter than a top. What's wrong?"

Wrong? "Nothing."

Gray arched an eyebrow, silently calling bullshit.

Not that she was going to tell him the truth. When she'd insisted she was going with him, she hadn't completely thought through the implications. It was one thing to be cooped up in the same office with him for ten hours a day, but to be a shadow at his side for the next several days…

At least back in Charleston she had the ability to go home and clear her mind of him. Or attempt to.

"Remind me again, why are we staying so long?"

Another expectation blown to bits. She'd assumed they'd fly up, track down his birth mother and head home. A day at the most. Instead, Gray had told her to pack enough for three or four days. Considering they already had a full rundown on his mother's information, including where she worked and lived, Blakely wasn't entirely certain what he expected to take so long.

"There are a couple other people I want to pay a visit to while we're here."

Blakely couldn't help the suspicion that snaked through her system. She'd been reading enough about Gray's history before he'd gone to prison to know that he'd spent quite a bit of time in Vegas before. And most of that time revolved around gambling, sex and outrageous benders that went on for days.

None of which she was interested in being a part of.

Sure, Gray hadn't done any of those things since he'd been out—at least not to her knowledge—so she didn't think that's what he had in mind, but…

"I'm not down for some wild Vegas weekend, Gray. I'm not interested in the lavish parties or high-roller games."

"Good, since neither of those things are on the

agenda. I simply want to check in with some people I used to know."

Blakely's eyes narrowed. Gray looked entirely sincere, his steady gaze holding hers as she watched him. Every fiber of her being wanted to believe him. But she couldn't completely shut down the sneering voice in the back of her head.

She finally shrugged and said, "Great, then I'll leave you to it and take a commercial flight home after we've talked with your mom."

"Nope. I need you here for my meetings."

"Why?"

"Because I'm talking to my former bookie, Surkov."

Nope, that did not sound like something she wanted to be involved with. "You don't need me to gamble."

"Do I look like an idiot to you?"

Blakely didn't understand the question, and seemingly unconnected segue, but answered, anyway. "No."

"Apparently I do if you think I'm here to place a bet. The main reason I spent seven years in prison is because I had a gambling habit. By no means was I an addict, but I wasn't exactly careful, either."

"Why'd you do it? The prosecution's biggest argument was that you were up to your eyeballs in debt to some bad people and didn't want to confess to Daddy to bail you out."

Gray's eyebrows rose. "And what do you think about that now?"

Blakely cocked her head and considered her answer for several seconds. What did she think? At the time, the only information she'd had about Gray was either what the media had told her or based on the limited interactions she'd witnessed at Lockwood Industries, which hadn't exactly painted Gray in the best light.

There was no doubt in her mind the man she knew now wouldn't have hesitated to do or say anything he needed to, including talking to his father, even if their relationship was strained.

But that didn't mean the man he'd been before would have reacted the same way. In fact, she was pretty certain the time he'd spent in prison had fundamentally changed him. And maybe for the better.

"I think I don't know who you were back then, so I can't really say. But I have a pretty good grasp of who you are now, and I don't think you'd be concerned about your father's reaction to anything."

"That's very true."

"However, after pouring over your personal financial records for the last week, I'm well aware that you had more than enough assets to cover the gambling debts without consulting your father."

"Also true."

"But that does raise the question—why did you routinely take out loans in order to gamble?"

Gray frowned and looked away for several seconds. "Because I was young, stupid and lazy."

"Well, doesn't that just explain all sorts of decisions we've all made."

Gray chuckled. "I was spoiled and used to getting

what I wanted immediately. On several occasions I found myself in Vegas, enjoying some high-stakes games, and ran out of liquid cash. It's easier to take out a high-interest loan in the middle of the night than contact my portfolio advisor to liquidate assets. Especially when I knew I had the ability to pay back the principal before the interest skyrocketed."

"But the last time...you didn't pay it back immediately."

"No, I didn't. Because my life got blown to bits when officers barged into my home to arrest me for embezzlement. I was a little preoccupied with clearing my name to worry about the latest loan. If I'd known it would be used against me, I would have taken care of it immediately. But, once again, I was spoiled and didn't give a shit. Not even when the gentleman who'd loaned me the money sent an envoy to impress upon me the need to make good on it."

Was he really saying what she thought he was? "They sent someone to rough you up?"

Gray's laughter filled the cabin. "You've been watching too many movies, Ms. Whittaker."

"No, I grew up around organized crime, Gray. I've seen plenty of despicable men do despicable things. Beating someone up over money would be mild in comparison."

Gray's sharp gaze cut to hers and Blakely realized just how much personal information she'd revealed. Personal information she hadn't meant to share with anyone, especially Gray Lockwood. The last thing she wanted was for him to feel sorry for her. Or, worse, ask for more details.

But he didn't. "They actually did just come to have a conversation. At the time, I thought because they knew I was good for the money. I'd paid in full before. But now…"

It wasn't hard for Blakely to connect the dots to what Gray might be thinking.

"Do you really think they had something to do with the embezzlement?"

Gray shrugged. "Logically, it doesn't make much sense. They knew I was good for the money."

No—no, it didn't. But then sometimes crazy people did asinine things.

"It's worth double-checking, though. Especially since we're in town. Turning over all the stones…"

Eight years too late. The guilt she'd been fighting for the last several days swelled inside her. The more she learned about Gray, the more certain she was that he was innocent. Which meant she'd played an instrumental part in sending an innocent man to prison for a significant chunk of his life.

And there was nothing she could do to make up for that.

It was her turn to apologize for something she couldn't change. "I'm sorry."

Gray shrugged, not even attempting to pretend he didn't know what she meant. "Not your fault."

That's where he was wrong, but she wasn't going to argue with him about it. She was going to protest staying, though.

"Considering you don't really expect it to be any-thing, you don't really need me here for this." Which meant she could escape, and maybe, just maybe, pre-vent herself from doing something stupid.

Like throwing herself at him and begging him to kiss the hell out of her again.

"Talking to my bookie? I don't."

Well, she hadn't expected him to agree with her. That was easy. Too easy.

Reaching across the aisle, Gray ran his fingers down a strand of Blakely's hair, sending a cascade of tingles from her scalp down to her toes.

"I want you here for me."

Seven

He'd made her nervous, which was actually a little cute. Mostly because from his observations, not much made Blakely Whittaker nervous. He was learning that she might appear small and fragile, but she had a core of straight-up steel.

It was one of the most attractive things about her. Although, he wasn't thrilled knowing she'd built that tough core because of the things she'd seen and experienced in her life.

It was still cute. He liked knowing he could make her off-kilter. Because she certainly had the ability to set his own life on its head.

It might be seriously inconvenient to be dealing with this now, but if there was one thing he'd learned in the last few years, it was that one couldn't control everything. Sometimes, one simply had to roll with the punches, enjoy the experiences and find the lessons.

And like he'd said earlier, he wasn't stupid. When faced with the opportunity to follow a couple of leads and spend several days in close quarters with Blakely... This was one of those times to take advantage of the opportunities.

Gray breezed through check-in at their hotel, going straight to the penthouse suite. It might have been several years since he'd visited, but the staff was fully aware of who he was and they'd been more than happy to accommodate his last-minute requests when he'd contacted them.

After punching in the code for the private elevator, he led Blakely into the small space. The minute the doors closed, he reached for her. Pulling her tight against his body, he backed them both up until she connected with the shiny chrome wall.

But he didn't kiss her. Yet.

Instead, his gaze raced around her face, taking in her wide, surprised expression. Her soft pink lips parted and a puffed gasp of breath caressed his face.

But she didn't move to break free. Instead, her hands settled at his hips, curling in and pulling him closer. Her pupils dilated as she leaned into him.

She wanted this as much as he did, which was all he needed to know.

Cupping a hand around the nape of her neck, Gray tilted her head and pulled her mouth to his. She tasted like peppermint and sin.

He tried to ease into it, to let them both sink into the connection, but Blakely had something else in mind. With a muffled groan, she rolled up onto her toes, trying to get more. One leg hooked over his hip, widening her stance so he could sink into the welcoming V of her open thighs.

Her heat and scent melted into him as she yanked him closer, grinding his hips against hers. Hers rolled, stroking his throbbing erection through the layers of their clothes.

She was hot as hell. And no doubt someone in security was enjoying the free show. As much as his body begged him to pull off all her clothes and take what she was clearly willing to give, he wasn't thrilled with the idea of having an audience the first time he stripped her naked and feasted on her delectable body.

Reluctantly, Gray put some space between them. But he couldn't make himself completely let her go. His hand still wrapped around her neck, he pressed his forehead against hers.

There was something calming and enticing about the way her body reacted to him. Labored breaths billowed in and out of her lungs, as if she'd just run a marathon instead of kissed the hell out of him. Which was good, since she made him feel the same way—as if he'd had the wind knocked out of him.

Her body arched, trying to find the connection again.

"Shhh," he whispered, nuzzling his lips against her forehead. "If I keep kissing you, I'm not going to be able to stop myself from pulling every stitch of your clothes off. And as much as I want that, the eye in the sky is always watching."

Blakely jerked and then stilled. After several seconds she whispered, "What are we doing? This isn't smart."

A puff of silent laughter escaped his lips. "Enjoying each other's company?"

"We don't like each other."

"You keep saying that. I like you just fine, Blakely. You're sharp, tough and resourceful. You're loyal to a fault and sexy as hell."

Brushing a strand of hair away from her face, Gray stared down at her as she stared up. Both of them paused, teetering on the edge of something. A choice. Potential. An opportunity that could be everything… or nothing more than a few stolen days of a good time.

Gray wasn't sure what would happen, but he knew without a doubt he was willing to take the chance to find out. He'd spent years without choices, without the option of doing and having what he wanted. Tonight, he was damned and determined to take the opportunity in front of him.

But only as long as Blakely wanted the same thing.

"When this elevator stops, I'm going into that room. If you follow me, I'm going to strip you bare, kiss every inch of your naked skin and fuck you until we're both blind with pleasure. If you're not okay with that, don't get off."

Blakely pressed a palm against the cold wall of the elevator. Gray didn't bother turning around to see if she followed when he exited. Was that because he knew she'd follow?

His words rang through her head. There was no question that she wanted what he was offering. Her entire body hummed with the aftermath of that kiss. She could feel the echo of his hands on her skin and needed more.

Following him wasn't smart. It wasn't safe.

But she was tired of being both. God, she'd been smart and safe her entire life. Played by the rules and watched as others who didn't were rewarded. Tonight, she wanted to feel. Real and raw. For once, she wanted to make a stupid, amazing, earth-rocking choice.

The aftermath would come soon enough.

The doors began to shut. Blakely's belly dropped to her toes, as if she'd already taken an express ride back to the bottom floor.

No.

Her hand shot out with inches to spare. The doors touched her skin and immediately bounced back. She slipped through the opening and into the entryway of an amazing suite.

A high ceiling soared above her head. And a massive wall of windows greeted her from the opposite side of the room. Taking several steps, Blakely surveyed the amazing view, a backdrop of light and action against the inky night sky.

Her breath backed into her lungs. Not because of the stunning view, but because Gray stepped up behind her.

The hard length of his body pressed against her.

His arms wrapped around her and his palm found the edge of her jaw. Gently cupping her face, he eased her around until his mouth found hers again. The angle of his hold had her arching against him, a little off balance and dependent on him for stability.

Something about that felt uncomfortable and inviting all at once. Because she knew there was no way he'd let her falter.

He held her exactly where he wanted, commanding the moment in a way that made the blood in her veins thick with anticipation. His other hand was busy, as well, methodically popping open the buttons down the front of her shirt.

She'd been purposeful when she'd dressed this morning. Casual, but professional. Determined to set the tone of this trip from the outset.

Spreading open her blouse, Gray let her mouth go long enough to peer at what he'd revealed.

"Please tell me your panties match this bra."

A small smile tugged at Blakely's lips.

She might have been professional on the outside, but staring at her lingerie options this morning, she just hadn't been able to make herself reach for anything plain. Instead, she'd chosen a mesh-and-lace bra that left almost everything except the bottom edge of her breasts naked. What was that saying? Something about sexy lingerie making a woman feel confident, even if no one else knew she was wearing it?

She'd embraced that school of thought for sure.

"As a matter of fact, they do." Maybe she was

gloating. A little. But the appreciation and approval in Gray's voice was absolutely worth it.

"Let me see."

Setting her away from him, Gray took several steps backward.

Turning, Blakely did the same, increasing the space. Without the pressure of his body to keep it in place, the shirt he'd opened slithered off her shoulders to pool at her feet.

Normally, Blakely felt uncomfortable in these types of situations. She was typically a get-naked-get-in-bed-and-have-sex kind of girl. Focused on the end result, because that's what they both wanted, right?

Tonight was entirely different.

Probably because of the way Gray was watching her.

His hungry gaze tripped across her skin. She could feel it, as tempting as any caress. Clearly, he wanted her. Appreciated her. Which only increased her confidence.

"I'm dying here, Blakely. Show me."

Reaching down, she popped the button and zipper on her pants. Rolling her hips, Blakely let them follow the shirt down to the ground.

Gray's sharp intake of breath was worth a million words. His deep green eyes went hot. Kicking off her heels, Blakely stepped closer, standing before him in nothing but her bra and panties.

Her nipples ached and her sex throbbed. She wanted him to touch her. A cool draft of air kissed her overheated skin, sending a scattering of goose bumps across her body.

"Gorgeous. You're beautiful, Blakely."

Closing the space between them, Gray cupped the nape of her neck and gently pulled her up onto her toes. He eased her into the towering shelter of his body, fusing their mouths together.

The kiss was powerful, deep. Drugging.

Languid desire melted through Blakely's body. His clothes scraped against her naked skin, reminding her how vulnerable she was right now. A dangerous edge of anxiety swirled at the fringes of the heat he was building.

Pulling back, she reached for the hem of his shirt, tugging it out of his slacks. Gray let her, somehow sensing her need to even the playing field. Lifting his arms, he helped her work the shirt up and off. Blakely didn't even bother tossing it—she simply let it drop to the floor behind him.

His ruffled dark brown hair made her lips curl up in a smile. Gray Lockwood wasn't the kind of guy who let much of anything ruffle him. It felt intimate somehow, to see him that way. More intimate than standing in front of him in her underwear.

Reaching for him, Blakely let her fingers sift through it, smoothing his hair back down. She let her hands drift down his neck, shoulders, torso.

Everything about him was tight and hard. His body swelled with muscle that had not been built in a gym. But what gave her pause was the smattering of scars scattered across his body.

Blakely let her fingertips play over them, memorizing the way the puckered skin felt. Gray stiffened beneath her exploration, but didn't pull away. She wanted to ask the questions, but knew he really didn't want to answer them.

And now wasn't the time.

Turning her gaze up to his, she leaned forward and placed her mouth over a particularly ugly one just over the swell of one of his pecs. And then let her mouth trail downward until she found the tight, tiny nub of nipple.

Sucking it into her mouth, Blakely relished Gray's groan. His fingers tangled in her hair, curled into a fist. His hold arched her neck at the same time he pressed into her. Blakely responded with the scrape of her teeth against the distended bud of flesh.

But that patience didn't last long. With a growl, Gray grasped her around the waist and boosted her up onto a kitchen island she hadn't even noticed was there.

The cold surface of the countertop connecting with the warm curve of her ass made her gasp with surprise. Reaching behind her, Gray had the clasp of her bra popped open and his mouth on her breast within seconds.

She arched into him, relishing the way Gray's wet mouth sucked on her skin. His palm spread wide at the base of her spine, keeping her where he wanted. Waves of sensation built in her belly as he tugged and sucked and laved.

His mouth played across her skin. Tingles chased

up and down her spine. Pressing her knees wide, Gray stepped into the open V of her thighs. His fingertips caressed the delicate skin at the juncture of her hip and thigh, tracing the edge of her panties. Teasing, tempting her with what she really wanted.

She writhed beneath his touch, needing so much more. "Please."

Gray obliged, slipping a finger beneath the barrier of her panties and finding the moist heat of her sex. Blakely gasped and arched up into his caress, silently demanding more.

"God, you're wet," he groaned.

Urging her down, Gray hooked his fingers into the sides of her panties and tugged them down her legs. Kneeling at her feet, he stared up at her. The expression on his face sent her reeling. Harsh, needy and sexy as hell. She'd never had a man look at her with such desire and intensity.

Naked, spread across the kitchen island, Blakely should have felt exposed. But she didn't. Instead, she felt empowered and sexy.

Hands to her knees, Gray urged her wider as he leaned forward to trail kisses up the expanse of her inner thigh. He licked and nipped, sucked and nuzzled. Until his wicked mouth found the very part of her aching for relief. Blakely's world went dark as his mouth narrowed everything down to that one spot.

His mouth was magic. Blakely groaned, dropping back on her elbows because her body just wouldn't stay upright anymore. Her eyes slipped shut, bursts of color flashing across her brain along with his light-ning strokes of pleasure.

The orgasm slammed into her, rocking her entire body. Her hips bucked against him, but his hard hold on her thighs kept her in place. She rode out the re-lentless waves for what felt like an eternity.

Blakely was breathing hard, her entire body labor-ing to pull enough oxygen into her lungs. Her elbows were shaky, but somehow she managed to stay mostly upright. It would have been embarrassing to collapse completely onto the kitchen counter in front of him.

Although, he probably wouldn't have cared.

Gray rose between her spread thighs. His mouth glistened with the aftermath of her orgasm. His own lips curled up into a self-satisfied smirk. Blakely had the urge to do whatever it took to wipe that expres-sion off his face.

Starting with stripping him of the last of his clothes.

Blakely curled her hands into the waistband of his slacks, using the hold to jerk him closer. Sitting up, she made quick work of his fly and pushed both the pants and boxer briefs over his hips.

Gray toed off his shoes and stepped out of the pile of clothing, kicking it out of the way.

God, he was gorgeous. Light spilled over his body, highlighting the peaks and valleys of pure muscle. Two grooves sat at the edge of his hips, leading with a V straight to the promised land.

His erection, long and thick, jutted out from his body. A tiny pearl of moisture clung to the swollen tip. Blakely's tongue swept out across her bottom lip. She really wanted to taste him.

A groan reverberated through the back of his throat. "Don't look at me that way."

Startled, Blakely's gaze ripped up to his. "What way?"

"Like I'm a chocolate sundae and you're starving."

A grin played at Blakely's lips. "You're better than a sundae, Gray, and you know it. You're hot as hell."

"You think so, huh?"

Shaking her head, Blakely gestured for him to come closer. "You're walking, talking sin. Shut up and come here."

Gray did what she demanded, stepping back between her open thighs. Blakely started to jump down from the counter, but the solid wall of his body prevented her.

Shaking his head, Gray said, "That's where I want you."

You'd think, considering she'd just had a mind-blowing orgasm, that she might have been a little more malleable and accommodating. Not so much. "Maybe I want to be somewhere else." Like on her knees with him in her mouth. That's really what she wanted.

"Too bad."

Perhaps if she told him her plan he would relent. But she never got the chance. Because the ability to speak left her the minute his fingers found her sex and plunged deep. A strangled sound stuck in the back of her throat and her hips jumped forward, pressing tight against his hand in an effort to get more.

"God, you're so tight."

She nodded, her brain unable to form any other coherent response. Gray's fingers worked in and out, stroking deep. Blakely's brain scrambled, emptying of every thought except for the pleasure he was giving her.

Her body went white-hot as her hips pumped in time with his fingers. She was so close…and then he simply stopped. With his fingers still buried deep in her pussy, he gave a come-hither motion with his other hand that had her eyes crossing.

"Holy…"

"My thought exactly," he said. "Lean back, open the drawer behind you and grab a condom."

Blakely blinked, but did as he asked. Rolling onto one elbow, she reached to the far side and pulled out a drawer. Sure enough, a pile of condoms sat there.

Grabbing one, she asked, "How'd you know?"

"Not my first time staying in this suite."

Blakely tried not to let his statement derail her. She didn't want to think about him being up here with another woman. Or women.

"And I might have asked the concierge to stock all the rooms with condoms."

Laughter and irritation bubbled up inside her chest. "Asshole."

He shrugged. "I believe in being prepared."

Apparently. Sitting back up, Blakely ripped into the package. Gray held out his hand for the condom, but she shooed him away. This was something she wanted to do.

Reaching for his hips, she guided him closer. Wrapping a hand around the long shaft of his sex, she relished the weight and size of him. Heat seeped into her palm. Friction added to it as she slid her hand up and down the length of him several times.

Blakely relished his groan and the way his hips thrust into her strokes. The walls of her own sex contracted. She wanted to feel him deep inside.

She rolled down the condom over his length and positioned him at the opening to her body. Hands on her hips, Gray paused, holding them both still.

Looking deeply into her eyes he said, "I'm sorry."

"For what?"

"It's been a while. This is probably going to be fast."

"How long is a while?"

"Almost eight years."

"Nope." No way was that possible. Sure, she understood why he was celibate for seven years, but he'd been out of prison for almost a year. Was it really possible he hadn't been with anyone that entire time?

"Why would I lie about something like that?"

He wouldn't. There was no reason to. "That's not what I meant. I just…find it hard to believe someone as handsome and sexual as you has chosen to be celibate."

"I was indiscriminate when I was younger. The past several years taught me what was important.

And I haven't found anyone I wanted to be with…
until now."

Blakely had no idea what to make of that, but she
really didn't have time to consider because Gray took
that moment to thrust home.

Blakely's head dropped backward. Her eyes slid
closed as she savored the indescribable feel of him.
Gray gave her a few moments to adjust.

Hands on her hips, he held her firmly in place as
he thrust. In and out, Gray set a pace that had tension
and pleasure building steadily inside her.

Sex on the kitchen counter in a penthouse suite
should have felt decadent and dangerous. Something
completely out of her normal life. And in some ways
this moment with Gray did feel like that. Eight years
ago, if someone had told her she'd be here with Gray,
she probably would have laughed in their face.

But now…

Blakely's hands ran across his body, touching,
memorizing, exploring. He was buried deep inside
her, and still she wanted him closer. Needed more
of him.

This wasn't just physical, although there was no
doubt they generated plenty of heat together.

Gray's mouth found hers, fusing them together in a
way that mimicked the connection of their bodies. His
tongue stroked deep inside even as his sex sank deep.

She felt the flutter of another orgasm teasing at
the edges of her senses. Gray's thrusts became harder
and deeper, his grip on her hips holding her tightly
in place.

And then the world burst open around her again. Just as he let out a roar of relief. His body shuddered against hers. And somehow she found the brainpower to wrap her arms around him and hold him tight. Together, they collapsed, the edge of the kitchen counter the only thing keeping Gray upright.

His labored breaths panted in her ear. The room around her slowly started to come back into focus. And, eventually, Gray pulled away.

She expected him to say something smart. To make some quip to cut the tension and make light of what had just happened between them. Because that's what she needed to keep her head on straight.

Instead, Gray smoothed a hand over her face. He cupped her jaw and brought her close.

"That was everything I ever imagined and more."

Blakely's chest swelled and something soft fluttered deep inside her belly.

But the feeling didn't last long. How could it when he looked at her, his intense gaze trained solely on her and filled with a heat that nearly singed her skin.

"But I'm nowhere close to done with you tonight."

Eight

One night was clearly not enough time with Blakely. Even if that one night had been the best sex of his life…and that was saying a lot.

As closed off as Blakely was in her regular life, she was just as open and free in the bedroom. It was a surprising discovery. One he was grateful for.

But as much as he'd love to take advantage of their surroundings by keeping her in bed all day, that wasn't an option.

Trailing his lips down the curve of her naked spine, Gray murmured, "Rise and shine, sleepyhead."

With a groan, Blakely buried her head farther under the pile of pillows she'd burrowed beneath. An unintelligible mumble floated up from the mound, but he got the gist of it.

"We don't have a few more minutes to spare."

He'd already let her sleep in. After grabbing the pillow shielding her face, Gray threw it onto the floor beside the bed.

Rolling his way, she cracked open a single eye and glared at him. "Go away."

Who knew she could be so cute in the morning?

Grabbing the mug of coffee he'd set on the bed-side table, Gray waved it beneath her nose. "I will, if you really want me to. But I'm pretty sure you were adamant about going with me yesterday."

"What kind of monster sets a meeting for the butt crack of dawn?"

Gray chuckled. "It's almost noon."

Blakely bolted upright. If he hadn't acted fast, her elbow would have connected with the mug in his hand, sending hot coffee flying across the bed.

"You're kidding."

"I'm not."

"Why'd you let me sleep this late? I never sleep this late."

Which was one reason he'd done it. He hadn't needed her to tell him to know she wasn't normally the type to sleep in. Blakely was a meet-the-day-at-dawn-and-work-until-well-into-the-evening kind of woman.

But it was also clear she wasn't used to staying up until almost two having sex.

"Letting you sleep was the least I could do after last night."

Blakely's gaze narrowed. Obviously, what he'd thought was a cute quip had hit her entirely wrong.

"Sleep for sex?"

"Uh, no."

Her gaze ran up and down his body, a confusing mixture of heat and disdain filling her eyes. "You obviously didn't feel the need to sleep in."

He'd gotten up a couple hours ago, showered and been handling a few things. "I don't sleep much."

Normally, he would have left the statement as it was, but for some reason more words followed. "Before prison I easily slept until past noon every day because I was up half the night. In prison…everything you do is regimented and controlled by the clock. They tell you when to sleep, eat and even go outside. I have a hard time sleeping in now, even when I want to."

The hard edge that had tightened Blakely's features eased. She collapsed back against the pile of pillows, her mouth twisting into a self-deprecating grimace. "I'm sorry."

"For what?"

"Waking up defensive. I'm not used to this."

Well, that had been obvious without the confession.

"I don't know how I'm supposed to act or what you expect."

Gray set the mug on the bedside table. Shifting, he sat on the bed and settled his hip into the curve of her waist.

"Blakely, I don't expect anything. And the only way you're supposed to act is whatever way feels right to you. You and I get to decide what we're doing and what we want from each other. Nothing else matters."

Her head tipped sideways as she considered him. "You're not at all what I thought."

"You've said that before."

"But I keep getting reminded."

Shifting higher against the headboard, she grasped the covers and tucked them beneath her arms, leaving her shoulders and collarbone bare.

What he really wanted to do was pull them back down again, lean forward and feast on her ripe breasts. Instead, he grabbed the coffee and held it out to her again.

Grasping the mug between her palms, she held it up to her face and pulled in a deep breath. Her eyes closed in bliss, her expression making his half-hard erection stir. She'd looked the same last night when he'd put his mouth on her.

Clearly, she liked her coffee. The look of surprise she sent him when she finally took her first sip was totally worth the extra effort he'd taken to make it just the way she liked it.

"How'd you know?"

Gray didn't pretend not to know exactly what she was asking. Shrugging, he said, "We've been working pretty closely together for the last week. I paid attention."

Her lips twisted into a wry smile. "I didn't."

"That's okay."

"No, I'm starting to realize it isn't."

Leaning forward, Blakely set her mug back on the

bedside table. Rolling up onto her knees, she let the covers pool at her waist. "How much time did you say we have?"

"Not enough."

Her hands roamed over her naked body, kneading her breasts. The tight bud of her nipples peaked between her spread fingers. "You're sure?"

Gray groaned. He wanted to be the one touching her. "Unfortunately, I am." Grasping her wrists, Gray pulled her hands away. Leaning forward, he laved one nipple, the rough scrape of his tongue across her soft flesh sending a sharp spike of need through him. "But, trust me, I have plans for you later, Ms. Whittaker."

"Oh, you do, do you?"

"Absolutely."

After a weird and unusual day, Blakely found herself back at the hotel, sitting on the couch with her feet curled up underneath her. She was reading through several emails that had come through on her Stone Surveillance account. Surprisingly enough, she was starting to feel like a real member of the team. In fact, one of the other investigators had sent her a request to review some financial documents on another case.

The case was simple and it had taken her less than an hour to look at what he'd sent…but it was interesting. And when she'd been able to send back a message with her insight, she'd felt like she'd contributed to something important.

That hadn't happened in a very long time.

She was just shutting down her computer when a loud knock on the door startled her. The sound reverberated through the huge suite, reminding her just how alone she was right now. After they'd returned from the meeting with Surkov—which had been unproductive, to say the least—Gray had left her in the suite to "run a couple errands," whatever that meant.

Unfolding from the sofa, Blakely padded across the room, the marble floor cool against the soles of her feet.

"Who is it?" she asked, looking through the peephole. Unfortunately, all she could see was a cart full of bags and boxes and a pair of shiny shoes sticking out from the bottom.

"Ms. Whittaker? Mr. Lockwood sent up some clothes for you from the boutiques downstairs."

Why would he do that? She had a suitcase filled with perfectly good clothes.

Opening the door, Blakely was already shaking her head. "I'm sorry to waste your time, but I don't need anything."

A petite woman stuck her head around the side of the cart and gave her a disarming smile. "He said you'd say that."

"Did he now?" Blakely wasn't certain what to think about that.

The woman nodded, her bangs flopping into her eyes. With a puff of breath, she blew the hair back out again, uncaring where the strands landed or how they looked. "He also said I wasn't allowed to leave until you let me inside. And he promised me a huge tip. Like a-week-of-salary huge, which I really need. So, please? Let me in?"

Blakely eyed the other woman. She couldn't be more than five-two, a hundred and ten pounds. Her face was round, but skinny. Her features were petite and yet somehow inviting. Maybe it was the disarming, begging smile that stretched her wide mouth. Or the contagious sparkle of excitement in her brown eyes. Either way, she was hardly threatening.

And there were logos from the shops Blakely had seen downstairs stamped on all the bags.

With a huff, Blakely pulled back and swept her arm wide, indicating the other woman should come in. Far be it for her to deny anyone a chance to make some money.

The other woman was practically bouncing as she wheeled the cart past Blakely. "I'm Desiree." With a grimace and a roll of her eyes, she continued, "Yeah, I know. It's awful. My mom was an eighties showgirl, convinced I was going to carry on the family legacy. To her utter shame, I have two left feet and about as much grace as a cactus."

Desiree pushed the cart into the center of the living room, stopped and took a quick turn around. "Nice." With a clap of her hands, she dismissed the opulence of the space and the amazing view outside the windows in favor of the loaded-down cart.

Tapping a finger against her lips, her eyes narrowed as she studied the things. Occasionally, she'd flip a considering glance over at Blakely.

"Not much to go on—"

"Hey!"

Desiree dismissed her indignation with a flip of her hand. "That's not what I meant. You're gorgeous. I meant I can't tell much about your personal style based on the oversize sweatshirt and bare feet you're currently wearing. I'm going to assume that's not your norm."

"You assume right."

"Mr. Lockwood gave me a few parameters and suggestions for what he'd like to see you in, but I'd like to get your input. Sure, we dress to impress the important man in our life, but you should feel amazing in it, too."

Was Gray the important man in her life? Blakely wasn't sure. Her libido definitely wanted a repeat performance of last night. And over the last week she'd come to realize, despite everything, that she might actually like the guy. But it was a huge leap from sex and mutual respect to him being the center of her universe.

A leap she was hardly ready to make.

"He's not important."

Desiree flipped her a disbelieving glance. "Trust me, I know people. He's important."

"Fine, but not to me."

Desiree gave her another expression that said "yeah, right," and shrugged. "If you say so."

"No, really. There's a lot you don't know about him. It's…complicated."

"Sister, it always is. Complicated makes life interesting."

"Interesting is dangerous."

Desiree shook her head. "Interesting is just interesting." Zipping open one of the bags, she revealed a sleek black jumpsuit. "Mr. Lockwood suggested you tend to wear very tailored clothing. Pieces that convey a sense of authority and control."

Interesting. Who knew he'd been studying her wardrobe? And apparently forming many opinions that he'd never voiced.

"He suggested you'd be most comfortable in something tailored and classic. But he also mentioned he'd like to give you the opportunity to try something new. To come out of your shell."

Come out of her shell? What did that mean? Was he passing judgment on her clothing choices? Blakely stared at the cart of things Gray had decided she needed to try.

Embarrassment and anger began to climb up her neck. "There's nothing wrong with the way I dress."

"Oh, I don't think that's what Mr. Lockwood meant."

"And just what did he mean?"

"He said he didn't think you'd had a lot of opportunity to indulge and play in your life, not even as a little girl. Which made me sad. I mean, every little girl should have a chance to play dress-up."

"So he wants me to dress up like a doll now?"

Blakely was lost, uncomfortable and out of her element. But she was also surprised because Gray had

pegged her pretty closely. She'd never been the type
to play in her mother's makeup or clomp around in
her heels. In fact, looking back, she couldn't remember a lot of laughter or happiness in her childhood.

It wasn't that she'd been miserable. Or mistreated.
There were plenty of kids who'd had it worse than
her, by far. But…

"I think he just wants you to have a chance to feel
beautiful."

Blakely blinked at Desiree. She couldn't remember
a single time in her life when she'd felt truly beautiful. The suits she preferred to wear to the office made
her feel powerful and competent. Prepared to handle
anything that came her way.

She hadn't even gone to her high-school prom.
Thinking back, she'd never actually owned a ball
gown. Or had a reason to want one. And she wasn't
exactly sure she wanted a fancy dress now. "I'm not
big on pink puffy dresses."

Desiree laughed, the warm, sultry sound surprising Blakely. She'd expected the tiny thing to have a
tinkly little laugh. "Good thing I don't have any of
those here, then."

With a twinkle in her eye, Desiree began to pull
several more outfits from their protective bags. One
was a dark red floor-length gown that would no doubt
cling to every curve she owned. And make her feel
like she was practically naked. Another emerald
green gown had a trumpet skirt that kicked out with
a row of ruffles.

Nope, neither of those were going to work.

Blakely's eye kept going back to the black jumpsuit Desiree had unwrapped first. It had a subtle sparkle to it and it had taken her several minutes to realize the satin material had iridescent threads running through it.

Desiree revealed a few more outfits, one off-white and another bright purple. There was no way she was wearing either of those colors. She swept her hands across the selection. "Pick your poison—which one do you want to try first?"

"The black one," Blakely stated without hesitation.

"Somehow I knew that's what you'd go for. Are you sure you don't want to try one of the others on just for fun?"

"Not on your life." Nothing about the others appealed to her.

"Okay." After pulling the jumpsuit off the hanger, Desiree handed it to her. "Just slip it on and I'll zip you up."

With a deep breath, Blakely disappeared into the bedroom. She pulled the sweatshirt over her head and dropped it to the floor. Turning her back to the doorway, she put one foot and then the other inside the garment. Pulling it up and over her shoulders, Blakely realized what had looked rather conservative on the hanger was actually sexy as hell. There was no back at all to the jumpsuit.

The waist cinched in, accentuating her hourglass figure. It rode high on her shoulders, cutting shallowly across her collarbone. The edge of the material fell away dramatically in a waterfall that pooled at the small of her back. The drape of the material hugged the curve of her ass and the deceptively long length of her legs.

Because the back was naked, she couldn't wear a bra. Her breasts swung free, brushing tantalizingly against the soft material with each deep intake of breath. She could already feel her body responding at the thought of wearing this in front of Gray.

Her nipples tightened and peaked, rubbing against the fabric.

Blakely reached up, covering both breasts and massaging in an effort to relieve the pressure.

"Well, that's a sexy sight to walk in on."

Blakely jumped and gasped at the sound of Gray's voice. She immediately dropped her hands as if she'd been caught doing something inappropriate.

"Oh, no, you don't. Put those hands right back where they were."

Blakely's gaze tore up to the mirror on the dresser across from her. Gray's penetrating gaze stared back at her, watching her with a predatory gleam that made the ache deep inside her ratchet higher.

He stood in the doorway, one hip propped against the jamb, head cocked to the side studying her. Both hands were tucked into the pockets of his slacks. He was deceptively calm even as his gaze ate her up. At some point he'd shed the suit jacket he'd been wearing earlier. The sleeves of his white dress shirt were rolled up his arms, revealing heavy muscle and bulging veins running up the length of his forearms.

He shut the bedroom door. "We're alone." A single

dark eyebrow winged up, silently demanding she do what he'd asked.

Slowly, Blakely's hands rose, settling back over her sensitive breasts.

"What were you thinking about?"

"You." The answer was simple and easy. But that's not what he was looking for.

"What about me? What had that look of pure pleasure crossing your beautiful face?"

There was something freeing about having the conversation through the reflection of the mirror. An added layer of distance that allowed her to be more open than she might have otherwise been.

"I was thinking about you taking me out of this outfit. Your mouth tugging on my swollen nipples. The scrape of the material across them was torture, so I was trying to ease the ache."

"Did it help?"

"Not really."

"Why not?"

"Because it wasn't what I wanted."

A smile played at the corners of his lush lips. "And what is it that you want?"

"You."

He shook his head. "You can do better than that."

"I want you to kiss me like you did last night. Like I was the air keeping you alive. I want you to run your fingers over every inch of my skin. I want your length buried deep inside me, stroking in and out until we're both panting from the need for relief."

Gray pushed away from the door, but his hands

stayed firmly where they were. Slowly, she watched him walk forward, closing the gap between them. Blakely's body reacted by drawing tight with anticipation. She wanted him to give her what she'd asked for.

Thinking that was exactly what he was going to do, she braced.

But he didn't. Instead, he sidled up behind her, bending his head down so he could rain kisses across the top of her shoulders. His hands settled on her hips for several seconds, holding her in place.

Slowly, his hands slid up her body, over her breasts and shoulders. One hand curled around her throat, his thumb placing pressure beneath her chin. The hold wasn't hard or demanding. In fact, it was soft and gentle.

He urged her attention to shift from watching his movements in the mirror to looking at herself.

At first, she was uncomfortable, her gaze continuing to slide away. But each time it did, the pressure of his thumb urged her back again. Finally, realizing the faster she complied, the faster he was going to let her go, Blakely gave in and did what he wanted.

"What do you see?"

"Me."

"Tell me more," he coaxed.

Blakely shrugged. "My hair's a mess. The jumpsuit is gorgeous, but not something I'd ever have a reason to wear again. I'm short and should have put on some makeup this morning. I look tired."

"You do look tired, but that's because you were up

half the night having passionate sex, which should be a good thing."

"It is a good thing."

"Then why do you say that with regret?"

Because she didn't like looking like something the cat had dragged in. Especially next to him. "You look like you've just stepped off the front cover of some men's fashion magazine. It isn't fair."

Gray chuckled. "I'll take that as a compliment."

Of course he would.

"Would you like to know what I see?"

"Yes."

No. Blakely's shoulders tightened. Did she really want to know?

"You're absolutely gorgeous, Blakely. Your skin is pale and perfectly soft. Those ice-blue eyes draw me in every time I look at you. But it's not just the unusual color. They're so bright with intelligence, curiosity and integrity."

"You mean judgment."

"I meant exactly what I said. Your messy hair reminds me that last night I was the one responsible for making it that way. I remember grabbing a fist of it and holding you exactly where I wanted you. And I remember that you let me. You're a damn strong woman, Blakely. I've known that from the first time we met. But last night…you felt safe enough with me to let go. Which only makes me want to give you more opportunities to do that."

"Is that what this is about?"

"What *what* is about?"

"The clothes?"

"Something like that. And we were invited to attend a VIP event at an exclusive club tonight. I thought it would be fun."

"You were invited." Blakely hadn't been invited to much of anything in her life, let alone a VIP Vegas party.

Gray shrugged. "Only because no one here knows you yet. You're beautiful, intelligent and forthright. Qualities most people appreciate. And when you decide to let go a little, you're amazingly fun. You're going to be a hit tonight."

Blakely scoffed. Now he was just blowing smoke up her ass.

"And with you wearing that outfit, I'm going to have to post a sign of ownership over your head to protect what's mine."

Blakely's eyebrows rose. "Buddy, I'm not yours or anyone else's. No one owns me."

Gray's mouth spread into a wide grin that crinkled the edges of his eyes. "I know. I just wanted to hear your response."

Nine

He was playing a dangerous game, but something told him it would be worth it.

For the past week Gray had studied Blakely. Even when he'd been trying to ignore her, he couldn't help himself. Which meant he'd learned a lot in those days.

But he'd learned even more about her last night.

Watching her relax and let go with him had been… perfection. A gift.

But it had also made him realize he wanted more from her than a stolen weekend in Vegas. However, he wasn't entirely certain she'd be open to the idea of actually being with him.

He hadn't really had a meeting this afternoon, just a need for some space to clear his head. At some point he'd come to the conclusion that it didn't particularly matter what Blakely thought she wanted—it was his job to convince her they could be real and more than just a few stolen moments, even if those moments had been combustible and amazing.

So he was on a mission to seduce her, not just physically, but mentally. And the first step of that was hopefully giving her a chance to loosen up and enjoy herself, something he didn't think she'd had the opportunity to do nearly enough.

Because he wanted to see more of that sparkle in her eyes. The wonder and relief. That easy smile—hard-won, but totally worth the effort.

And right now was the perfect opportunity.

Gray watched Blakely's reflection in the bedroom mirror. She was beautiful even before the team of makeup artists and hairstylists showed up in a bit to do their thing. He'd picked out the jumpsuit himself, knowing it would be perfect for her. He'd also instructed Desiree to give her several other options, just in case he'd been wrong.

But he hadn't been.

He also wasn't wrong that it would look amazing on her.

The outfit was pure class and sophistication, but with a touch of drama at the back. And he couldn't wait to get his hands on the gleaming expanse of satiny skin left bare.

If he touched her right now, though, they'd never leave the suite. And as tempting as that idea was, he wanted to give her a night out first.

"Relax, Blakely, and enjoy the experience."

"Easy for you to say," she grumbled.

"No, it really isn't," Gray countered, his voice filling with wry humor. There was a time in his life that putting on a tux and attending some fancy party was the norm. No, not just the norm. He'd felt a sense of entitlement to be invited. Like the world and everyone in it owed him simply because of who he was.

However, it had been a long time since he'd bothered to enjoy the kind of party they were going to attend. Oh, it would have been easy to revert to old bad behavior once he'd been released. Especially after his father and mother had looked him in the eye and told him they'd be happy to never see him again.

But his time in prison had made him stronger than who he used to be.

That didn't mean he wasn't looking forward to bringing a little glamour and sparkle into Blakely's life. Something told him she'd been seriously lacking in those two things for a very long time.

She might be severely out of her element, but she deserved to have a Cinderella moment.

"You've got about thirty minutes before the rest of the staff shows up to help you get ready."

"Staff? What the heck are you talking about?"

"Hair and makeup."

"You think I can't do my own hair and makeup?" Blakely asked indignantly.

"Of course I know you can. But most women find it fun to let someone else do those kinds of things occasionally."

"I'm not most women."

Gray closed the space between them. Hands to her shoulders, he spun her around so she was facing him. "Of that, I'm keenly aware," he murmured before dropping his head and finding her mouth.

The kiss was deep and hot, a blazing inferno within seconds. Touching her always made him want. Gray let the connection pull him in and under—he relished the taste and feel of her.

It would have been so easy to just give in and let the moment spin out of control. But, somehow, he found the strength to pull back. "Can you do me a favor?" he asked, staring deep into her pale eyes.

Expression glazed with desire and need, she mutely nodded. When she looked at him that way... it was hard to think about anything else.

"Stop fighting me and assuming the worst out of everything I do and say."

"I expect the worst."

A tight band squeezed around his chest. "I know."

Reaching up, he smoothed her soft hair away from the edge of her face. It really bothered him that she'd been taught by everyone in her life to be so wary, including the people who were supposed to protect her the most.

"I have only the best intentions where you're concerned, Blakely. You're a remarkable woman and I simply want to show you how much I value your company."

"I don't need expensive clothes and people waiting on me hand and foot."

No, she didn't. Most of the women who'd been

in his life would have accepted his gesture without comment. Hell, they would have expected it. But not Blakely. "Which is exactly why I want to give those things to you. Let me."

She blinked. Slowly, she nodded.

"Excellent. As much as I'd like nothing better than to strip you out of this outfit right now, that's going to have to wait until later. You have twenty minutes to shower before everyone gets here."

After spinning her away from him, Gray pushed her forward. She stumbled a step, but quickly found her footing. Shooting him a perturbed look over her shoulder, he couldn't help but take advantage of the perfect target in front of him.

Reaching out, he smacked her on the rear. "Hop to it."

Blakely yelped and glared at him. No doubt, he'd pay for that later, but he was looking forward to that, too.

Retracing his steps into the living room, he asked Desiree to leave all the accessories that matched the jumpsuit before dismissing her.

Dropping into a chair by the massive wall of windows, he ignored the spectacular view spread out before him. The city was alive with light and activity, but none of that interested him. Instead, he opened his email on his phone and began sifting through the business he'd been ignoring for most of the day.

The dead end with Surkov hadn't come as a surprise. And yet, he'd still left the meeting disappointed.

Because he really was no closer today to figuring out who had set him up than he'd been months ago.

The longer he went without a credible lead, the more nervous he was becoming. Because without understanding what had happened, who had set him up and what their motive had been, the possibility that it could happen again lurked around every corner. The damage to his life had blindsided him. And he was willing to do whatever was necessary in order to make damn sure it didn't happen again.

And now, Blakely was involved. Which could potentially put her at risk. A reality he did not like.

With a sigh, Gray zeroed in on the email from Joker that had come in several hours ago. Opening it up, he was hopeful until he realized it was a report on his birth mother, not anything to do with the embezzlement.

Reading the details about the woman who'd given birth to him, basically sold him and then attempted to blackmail his mother did not give him a warm, fuzzy feeling. Apparently, she'd continued to live a high-profile life here in Vegas. At least until the last few years, when her beauty and talent had begun to fade and she couldn't trade on them anymore to support her excessive lifestyle.

She'd gone from having her name featured on the marquee to being a nameless face in the background. Without even meeting her, he had a feeling that hadn't gone over well.

Not to mention, she'd apparently had connections with some questionable people over the years. Joker had discovered that her long-term boyfriend was a well-known criminal.

After reading the report twice, Gray finally closed the document and tossed his phone onto the table in front of him. Nothing inside him wanted to deal with the situation right now. Tomorrow would be soon enough to confront his birth mother and tell her the blackmail wouldn't work; she was going to have to find another cash cow to bankroll her high-roller tendencies.

With a sigh, Gray sank back into the chair. He rubbed his eyes, realizing they were gritty with fatigue for the first time since he'd gotten up this morning. Not surprising, considering he and Blakely had been awake half the night.

He must have fallen asleep, because one moment he was contemplating getting up and taking a shower so he could be ready whenever Blakely was, and the next she was leaning over him, shaking his shoulder and murmuring his name. "Gray…"

Slowly, he blinked his eyes open, his vision bleary and unfocused. A halo of light shone around Blakely's head, like the ring of light depicted in paintings of Mary. Her entire being glowed. It wasn't a description he'd normally use for Blakely. She was many things, but maternally divine wasn't one of them.

However, there was no debating that the glow came from deep inside her. She was radiant in a way that made him want to worship at her feet.

"Gray, are you okay?"

Slowly, everything came into focus. He sat up and

Blakely took several steps back, giving him a perfectly unobstructed view of her.

"You're breathtaking."

A deep blush crept up her skin. Clearly, she didn't receive enough compliments. He was going to have to remedy that.

But right now, he needed to get them out of this room, or all the effort the team he'd hired had put into Blakely's appearance would be wasted because they'd never leave the suite.

Standing, Gray texted their driver that they were on the way down, then slipped his phone into his pocket. He held a hand out to her and waited, slightly surprised when she actually twined her fingers with his.

He snagged his suit coat and led them out into the waiting elevator. Wrapping an arm around her, Gray used their joined hands at the small of her back to press her tight against his side. He loved the feel of her there. The way the lush curves of her breasts settled heavily against his arm. The subtle scent of her tantalized his senses. And he could feel the heat of her moist breath against his neck.

"Where are we going?"

"Excess—it's a club downtown."

"Sounds very Vegas."

Gray chuckled. "It's popular enough. I know the owner."

"Partied there often, did you?"

A wry smile tugged at his lips. "Something like that."

The ride in the car was quiet. Blakely would never be the kind of woman to fill a silence with chatter, which was something Gray happened to like about her. When she had something important or profound to share, she did it. Otherwise, she kept her thoughts to herself.

Which intrigued him. Because he really wanted to know what went on behind those intelligent, beautiful eyes.

The drive didn't take long. Less than twenty minutes later they were ensconced in the VIP area on the second floor, overlooking the bustle of the club and the main dance floor below. They had a private waitstaff, dancers and floor of their own.

Gray didn't bother to ask Blakely what she wanted, but ordered drinks for them both. His mission tonight was to get her loosened up enough to see her dance, something he'd hazard Blakely hadn't done much in her life.

A perfect reason for him to want to make it happen.

They'd been sitting there for about fifteen minutes when a heavy hand landed on his shoulder. Gray's heart raced and adrenaline shot into his system. He reacted, snapping a hand down over the wrist and barely checking himself before he could use leverage and power to break the person's arm and throw him over the back of the chair and onto the floor at his feet.

But he wasn't in the middle of a crude fighting ring.

Blakely sat forward, spilling her drink as she settled it on the table in front of them. She was halfway out of her seat, panic in her eyes, before he could stop her.

Shaking his head, he silently told her he was fine. Although, the hitch in his lungs suggested that might be a lie.

"Good to see you back here, my friend," a familiar voice, clearly oblivious to just how close he'd come to having his arm broken, rumbled from behind him.

Pulling in a huge gulp of air, Gray willed his body to settle. Pasting a smile on his face, he turned and stood in a fluid motion, dislodging the heavy hold from his shoulder.

Clapping a hand across Dominic's shoulder, he said, "It's good to be back."

Blakely's heart was still in her throat as Gray turned to make introductions.

She'd seen the look of shock and involuntary reaction before Gray had shut it down. His body tensed, every vein popping into relief down his muscled arms. His eyes had hardened, turning to the most cold and deadly emerald green she'd ever seen.

A part of her had always recognized Gray had a hidden edge of danger, but there was no doubt she'd almost gotten a firsthand introduction to it right now. Luckily, he had impeccable control over his physical reflexes.

For the first time, Blakely realized she was standing. Her fingers were curled around the edge of the table. Loosening her grip, she held out a hand to the man now standing beside Gray.

"Blakely Whittaker, meet Dominic Mercado."

Dominic leaned forward into the space between them. He grasped her hand in both of his, giving hers a squeeze instead of actually shaking it. "Please tell me you're willing to dump this asshole and spend the evening with me instead."

Gray lifted a single eyebrow. "I'm the asshole? You're the man hitting on my date right in front of me."

Dominic's eyes twinkled as he offered her a wide grin. "I've learned in life, it's folly to ignore the opportunities in front of you. And I'd kick myself if I let this vision walk away without at least taking a shot."

"Too bad for you, she's already taken."

This time, it was Dominic's turn to cock an eyebrow. "Perhaps you should let the lady speak for herself. Are you going to choose this scoundrel over an upstanding citizen and business owner like myself?"

Blakely's gaze bounced back and forth between the two men for several moments. They were clearly friendly, but with an undercurrent of rivalry running beneath their exchange.

Gray simply watched her, waiting for her reaction. Although, his gaze did narrow when it slipped down to take in the way Dominic still had a hold of her hand.

Finally, Blakely turned to Dominic. Tugging gently, she pulled out of his grasp.

"I'm flattered."

Dominic sighed and shook his head. "No, you're not."

Blakely rolled her eyes. "Gray isn't a scoundrel. And something tells me 'upstanding citizen' might be a stretch."

Dominic's grin widened. "Perceptive, isn't she?"

Gray's entire body relaxed. "That she is. Smart as hell, too."

"Lucky bastard."

"You have no idea." Holding out a hand, Gray pulled her into the shelter of his body and she accepted. "Thanks for the info I asked for."

Dominic gave Gray a smile, this one actually genuine. "You're welcome. Anything for you, man, although I don't understand why you're looking into Vegas showgirls with questionable taste in men. Please tell me you're not looking to invest in a show or something stupid."

"Nothing like that. I'm part owner in a surveillance company and she's connected to a case we're working."

Dominic's mouth curled into a grimace. "Not surprising. Her boyfriend has a nasty reputation and I wouldn't be surprised to find out she's up to her neck in the bad shit, too."

"There's plenty of that to be found in this town."

Dominic's gaze scraped over the crowd around them. "Isn't that the truth? Well, I'm going to go back behind the bar and appease my wounded ego with an expensive glass of single-malt scotch." Tipping two fingers to his forehead, he offered them a salute, then said, "Enjoy yourselves. Let my staff know if you need anything."

Gray nodded, his grip around her waist tightening as Dominic turned to leave. Blakely watched as he melted into the crowd, stopping at several tables to speak briefly to people here and there.

From out of nowhere, a tall redhead in a flashy sequined dress stalked up to him. Blakely couldn't hear their words over the roar of music, but clearly the conversation was heated. And the affable, charming, slightly smarmy persona Dominic had been wearing disappeared. His entire body language changed.

Wrapping a hand around her upper arm, he pulled her in so they were practically nose to nose. And then let her go again when she used her other hand to shove him away. Spinning on her heel, the redhead disappeared into the crowd.

And Dominic simply watched her go. But his hands were balled into fists at his sides and his chest heaved as he tried to get ahold of his response.

"Well, that was interesting."

Blakely's attention turned back to Gray. "How so?"

"The redhead? That's his little sister's best friend. I dated Annalise, his sister, for about two minutes when we were in our early twenties, which is how I met Dominic. Our friendship stuck when the relationship didn't. I didn't realize Meredith was still around."

Shaking his head, Gray's mouth twisted into a wry grimace. "I suppose a lot happened while I was gone. Not that it matters."

The techno music that had been blasting into the

space changed. The tempo slowed, even though there was still a thump of bass running beneath the sounds. Several people streamed off the dance floor as others moved on.

Gray didn't bother to ask as he tugged her onto the dance floor.

Grasping her hand, he spun her out and then pulled her back in. Her body settled against the hard planes of his. Thanks to last night, she knew intimately what his Greek-god body looked like beneath the sophisticated layer of his suit.

And she immediately wanted to experience that wonderland again. Her hand snuck beneath his jacket, sliding along the rough texture of his tailored shirt. His body heat warmed her palm. And she loved the way he arched into her touch. Her fingers found the edge of his slacks and teased down as far as they could go. Unfortunately, she couldn't quite reach the bare skin of his ass.

However, his hands could find naked skin. One palm spread wide at the small of her back. His own fingertips tantalized as they dipped into the opening just above the dint of her ass. Pulling her close, he folded his other hand between their two bodies, strategically using the cover of the dance to hide the fact that he was running a fingernail across the distended bud of her nipple.

"I'm pretty sure that's not playing fair," Blakely gasped.

Her entire body began to tingle.

"No, I'm pretty sure this jumpsuit isn't playing fair."

"You're the one who picked it out."

"True. Who knew I was into torture? Knowing you're wearing nothing under this thing has been driving me crazy all night."

Pulling back, Blakely stared up at Gray. "Remind me, why are we still here?"

A grin played at the edges of his lips. "That's a good damn question."

As much as Gray wanted to accept the dare in her heated gaze, there was something they had to do first.

"We have one more stop to make…it's time I met my mother."

Ten

Getting backstage had never been hard for him. Money and notoriety provided access to more than most people wanted to believe. His conviction hadn't simply made the local news, but had hit the national media circuit. On the heels of several high-profile financial scandals, his was just another in a trend...or that's how the media machine had spun it.

Which had pissed off his father. That man did not subscribe to the any-publicity-is-good-publicity mentality.

Gray would admit that for most of his life, walking through doors locked to everyone else gave him a small thrill. A sense of power, right or wrong. Tonight, his stomach just churned when the guard looked at the cash he'd slipped into his hand and then swept them past without so much as a change in his facial expression.

Several steps down the darkened hallway, Blakely pulled him to a stop. Her calming hand rested on his arm as she turned to face him.

"You okay?"

No, he really wasn't. Normally, he'd have kept that confession to himself, but for some reason Gray let the confession free. "I'm a nervous wreck."

A short burst of laughter shot between them. Okay, not the reaction he'd expected.

"You certainly don't look it. I'm starting to realize the calm, reserved exterior you show the world might hide a whole lot."

It was Gray's turn to chuckle, but Blakely wasn't wrong. Long before prison, his father had taught him emotions were something that made you weak. The world rewarded strength, even if it was a facade.

Gray could count on one hand the number of people who recognized that about him, though. And those people were all the most important ones in his life. The idea that Blakely could join that group…made him even more nervous than knowing he was about to meet Cece, his mother.

Leaning back against the wall, Gray wrapped his arms around Blakely and pulled her tight against his body. His mouth found hers in a brutal kiss that gave him the strength he needed.

The feel of her settled him. Centered him in a way only getting in the ring had done before. The way she opened to him, melted against him, made him feel powerful and protective. He let the moment spin, allowing the connection he felt with Blakely to overshadow everything else.

She was the one to finally break the kiss. Pulling back, she whispered, "We need to go."

Shaking his head, Gray knew she was right. But a huge part of him wanted to stay in this dingy hallway with her. To freeze this moment and hold on to it. Hold on to her.

Pressing his forehead to hers, Gray let his eyes drift closed. "Thank you for being here."

Her hands, resting on his hips, squeezed. "I wouldn't be anywhere else. You're not alone in this, Gray."

Damn, it had been a long time since he'd felt that was true. His parents, the people who were supposed to support him and love him unconditionally, had turned their backs when he'd needed them most. They'd believed the lies instead of him.

Sure, Stone and Finn had his back. Of that he was one hundred percent certain. Not just because they said they did, but because they'd proven it time and again. But they both had their own lives. They were married and were hip-deep in building Stone Surveillance. No doubt they'd drop everything if he needed them, but their focus shouldn't be his problems and his life.

And Blakely… Right now, she made him feel like he mattered. She was the most amazing woman he'd ever met, and if she could care about him, maybe that meant he was actually a good person, worthy of someone else caring.

Gray was about three seconds away from saying to hell with it and taking her home without doing what they'd come here to do, when a wolf whistle sounded from down the hall. "Get a room!"

A wry smile lit Blakely's ice-blue eyes as she pushed away from him. Her hand slid down his arm until her fingers were twined with his. She didn't wait for him, but used their connection to bring him along behind her as they continued down the hallway.

The mountain of meat at the door had told him Cece was in the second-to-last room on the left. The closer they got to that end of the long hallway, the more noise could be heard. The tinkle of laughter and rumble of voices. The ring of hangers against metal rods and the dull thud of things being dropped onto a wooden surface.

They passed one room that was occupied by a group of women. Glancing in, they were half-naked and didn't particularly care the door was standing wide open. Bright, naked bulbs ringed multiple large mirrors. Several women were leaning forward, applying makeup to their faces.

The cacophony didn't surprise Gray. It also didn't hold his attention for anything more than a passing glance. Blakely, on the other hand, slowed, her eyes glued to the sight. Her expression was blank and controlled, so he couldn't tell what thoughts were spinning behind her gorgeous eyes. If he had to guess, though, the thought of being half-naked in a room with twelve other women would give her hives. She wasn't exactly a prude, but she was fairly private.

Later, he'd ask. But right now, he was laser-focused on getting this over with. Something told him his mother wasn't likely to greet him with a teddy bear she'd been carrying around for the last thirty-four years hoping for the opportunity to give it to him.

He didn't live in a Hollywood movie. Not to mention, she'd sent a blackmail demand.

His nerves from before hadn't disappeared, but they'd been joined by a healthy ribbon of anger. Justified or not, it was there and if he wasn't careful, it might color the coming encounter.

The room that the security guy had directed him to was much different from the one they'd just passed. The door was closed, and there was no noise emanating from behind the solid surface.

Gray didn't bother knocking. He simply turned the old round knob and pushed.

The woman in front of the mirror on the far wall spun. Her face was ripe with surprise that quickly morphed into anger. Her eyebrows, clearly exaggerated with stage makeup, slammed down into an angry V.

Gray wasn't certain what he'd expected. Maybe to feel this cosmic connection. Or maybe experience a bone-deep recognition. But there was nothing. The woman looking back at him was a complete stranger.

Oh, certainly, he could recognize features of himself in her. The set of her mouth was familiar. The shape of her eyes, even if hers were brown while his were green. But that was it.

Dispassionately, Gray cataloged her as a woman. Clearly, she'd been beautiful once. Her skin was sagging and lined, but the array of jars behind her suggested she spent time and money to preserve what she could. Her hair was thick and shiny, and hung down her back in lush waves.

She'd also taken time and effort to keep her body in top physical shape. She was slender, and her collarbone jutted out.

Cece stood. The heavy wooden chair she'd been sitting in clattered to the floor. "What are you doing here?"

Gray reached behind him and closed the door. The quiet click reverberated through the room.

"You know who I am." Gray didn't bother to make the statement a question. It was clear from her reaction that she did.

"Of course I know who you are."

Gray huffed with sarcastic laughter. "There's no 'of course' about it, considering I didn't know you existed until two days ago."

"And whose fault is that?"

"I'm going to say yours since you sold me when I was just a few days old."

Her mouth twisted into a nasty expression, and suddenly, Gray realized she wasn't beautiful after all. It was a facade, like everything else about her. "Is that what he told you? Of course he made me out to be the bad guy."

"My father didn't tell me anything. How could he? He hasn't spoken to me in almost eight years."

Her eyes glittered with malice. "That bitch's account wouldn't be any better."

"I assume the bitch you're referring to is my mother."

"No, *I'm* your mother."

Her words made his stomach roll. Oh, he'd known they were true, but hearing her say them out loud, especially with a sneer in her voice, made him want to cringe. Or deck her. But he refused to do either.

"No, you're not. Neither is she, for that matter. But that's none of your business. I'm here to tell you the secret isn't a secret anymore. You can send threatening letters to whomever you'd like, but they're not going to do you any good. No one is giving you more money."

Cece slammed a container of makeup onto the table behind her. It exploded, a puff of powder raining over the surface. "I'm going to kill that little bitch if I ever find her."

Gray took a menacing step forward. Blakely's hand shot out, curling around his bicep and holding him in place. "Did you just threaten my mother?" She might not have been much of one to him, and certainly not when he'd needed her most, but he wasn't about to let this woman get away with threatening her anymore.

"No. I don't give a shit what your mother does. I'm going to kill your sister. Once again, she's managed to ruin everything and she isn't even here."

Out of all the revelations he'd gotten in the last few

days, those words actually rocked Gray's world. He went backward on his heels, as if he'd just received an uppercut to the jaw. If Blakely hadn't been standing behind him, he might have fallen to the floor.

"What sister?"

He had a sister.

A sneer twisted Cece's lips. "Half sister."

He had a sister.

"Where is she?"

"That's a damn good question. I haven't seen her in about eight years."

Was it a coincidence his sister had disappeared around the same time he'd gone to jail? Warning bells clanged inside Gray's brain.

"Why?"

Cece stared at him for several seconds, then said, "Screw it." She collapsed back into the chair. "Not much you can do about it, anyway."

Something told him he wasn't going to like whatever she had to say.

"The worthless little shit disappeared the same night she moved twenty million dollars into your bank account. She was supposed to move another twenty million into my account, but obviously that never happened."

His *sister* had set him up. A sister he never even knew existed.

Why? Why would she do that? What had he done that she'd wanted to ruin his entire life? And was she still a threat?

Gray's stomach clenched tight. This conversation had just taken a severe turn he'd not been prepared for.

"Why would she frame me for embezzlement?"

"She wasn't supposed to. She was supposed to frame your father. My guess is she screwed up and put the money into the wrong account. I didn't even know it had happened until the story hit the news and I realized the mess."

His father had been the original target? They did share a name. Gray was a nickname he'd used since he was a little boy. All of his accounts were obviously set up in his legal name, something he never thought of because he didn't actually use it.

"Why would she frame my father?"

"Because I'd hit a rough patch and he refused to help me out when I went to him."

"So you decided to rob him? What does that have to do with my sister?"

"Your sister is a computer genius. There isn't a system she can't access or a site she can't crash."

His sister was a hacker? And from what his mother said, a talented one.

"How'd she learn those skills?" That wasn't the kind of thing you were born instinctively knowing. Sure, certain people had an aptitude, but they still had to learn. Especially the illegal stuff.

"Michael, her father, recognized her talent when she was young. She was the kind of kid who'd spend hours taking apart the computer I bought her for Christmas just to see what the guts looked like and whether she could put them back together again. It didn't take long to figure out she was just as amazing at breaking codes." His mother shrugged her shoulders. "One puzzle is as good as another. He took her under his wing and trained her. She was seriously beneficial in his business."

His illegal business. Dominic had provided Gray with a bit of information about Michael when he'd passed along some details about Cece. While Joker had uncovered quite a bit, Gray had decided that getting insight from a local was just smart.

His mother had let her boyfriend use her daughter for criminal activity. Gray shouldn't be surprised, all things considered, but he was. "How old was she?"

"When she started?" She shrugged. "Seven or eight. When she screwed you? Sixteen."

Gray saw red. His mother had been exploiting his sister while she was too young to know better. She'd grown up committing crimes and didn't know any other life.

"Framing you was a mistake. She didn't even know you existed. But disappearing with my money—that was all planned."

No doubt. Gray couldn't help but be proud of his sister for her resourcefulness. Even if he'd been the one to pay the price with seven years of his life.

Although, that was assuming his sister wasn't aware of what she was doing. If she'd screwed him on purpose...

"You have no idea where she is?"

"If I did, do you think I'd have sent that note to your mom?"

No, she wouldn't.

Gray let his gaze drift up and down, taking in the woman who'd given birth to him. Even through the heavy makeup he could tell she was tired and worn. Her shoulders were slumped and the caked-on makeup had settled into the deep lines around her mouth.

The only word that came to Gray's mind was pathetic. She'd spent her life trading on her beauty to get what she wanted, but was clearly starting to realize external beauty faded. And now she was screwed because she didn't have a backup plan.

"Don't bother sending any more threatening notes. You won't be getting any more money from anyone in my family."

"I'll go to the media."

Gray shrugged. "Go ahead. Do you really think a thirty-five-year-old sex scandal will matter to anyone?"

Cece laughed, the sharp sound scraping across his eardrums. "Your name is still big in the media. They'll eat up the story."

"No one will care. I've been out of prison for almost a year. Hell, my parole is finished in a couple months."

Blakely's fingers squeezed his arm again. She hadn't said a single thing during the exchange, but he'd known she was right beside him.

"Go ahead. See how far that gets you. You can only sell the story once."

Gray took a few steps backward. The expression on Cece's face left his belly churning—not because he was concerned, but because she looked utterly devastated and broken.

But that wasn't his problem. She was no one to him.

His sister, on the other hand, was someone he wanted to talk to.

From across the aisle on the plane, Blakely watched Gray. He'd been quiet and distant since they'd walked away from his mother. At first, she'd worried he was about to lose it and tear into the woman. But she should have known better. Gray Lockwood had tight control, even in the midst of utter turmoil.

Hell, she was still trying to digest the information bomb his mother had dropped and it had nothing to do with her.

She'd been quiet for a while, but at some point, they were going to have to talk about it.

"What are you going to do?"

Gray turned to her, his gaze distant and unfocused. "What?"

"What are you going to do?"

His gaze sharpened. He blinked several times. "Find my sister."

Obviously, she never expected anything less. "Are you going to tell the authorities about Cece and her role in everything?"

With a sigh, Gray let his head drop back against the seat. Reaching up, he rubbed his fingers into his eyes. "No, I don't have any proof."

"You have me as a witness."

"Sure, and considering we're sleeping together, that'll go over well."

"No one knows."

Gray's hands fell into his lap. He stared at her for a few seconds. "At the very least, everyone knows we've been working closely together."

"Surely there's a way to make your mother and her boyfriend pay for what they did."

"I doubt it. It's not likely there's a trail to follow, but I'll have Joker see what he can dig up. At least now he knows where to look, which should help. But I'm going to assume they were very careful about getting their hands dirty. And without the trail of money to trace back to them…it's going to be difficult to prove."

"Your sister is the linchpin."

Gray's body sagged against the leather. "She is. I need Joker to track her, as well. Same thing, knowing where to start will hopefully make the job easier."

Maybe, but his mother had said *they* hadn't been able to find her for the last eight years. And something told Blakely they'd worked at finding her since the girl potentially had twenty million dollars.

Eight years of being missing—that was a long time. Blakely didn't want to say it out loud, but maybe she was dead. His sister had been sixteen, after all, when she'd disappeared. Even with twenty million, it must have been difficult to be on her own.

Blakely might have felt like her father had abandoned her, choosing his friends and a life that took him away from them, but at least she'd always had her mother to count on. To shelter and protect her. It sounded like Gray's sister hadn't had anyone to care about her. Blakely could hardly imagine the woman they'd seen tonight being anything close to maternal.

"When we get back, I'll tell Stone you're available for other assignments. I know he has a couple he could use your help on."

"No."

Gray's eyebrows beetled into a deep frown. "You're not still hell-bent on leaving Stone Surveillance, are you? Not only are you good at this kind of work, you enjoy it. Don't try to deny that."

Why would she deny it? "Yes, I really enjoy it. I enjoy putting the pieces together and solving the puzzle. I love feeling like what I'm doing might make a real difference to someone. But…"

"So why do you want to leave?"

"No one said anything about leaving. I'll stay as long as I have a job."

"I'm confused."

"My assignment with you isn't finished."

Gray shook his head. "Yes, it is. You agreed to help me figure out what happened. Now I know."

"Maybe, but the bread crumbs don't end there, do they? I owe you a hell of a lot. The least I can do is see this through."

"You don't owe me anything, Blakely."

That's where he was terribly wrong. She owed him seven years of his life, but there was no way she could give those back to him. "You're wrong. My testimony was key to putting you behind bars for a crime you didn't commit."

Gray opened his mouth to protest, but Blakely wasn't having any of it. Holding up a hand, she said, "Don't even bother denying it. We both know it's true. How do you think that makes me feel? Knowing I'm responsible for you losing seven years of your life? Being disowned by your family and barred from the company and your heritage?"

Instead of smoothing out Gray's frown, her words had the opposite effect. Dark anger swirled in the deep green depths of his eyes. "Do you think I want your pity?"

"No, so it's a good thing what I'm feeling is far from pity."

"Ha." Gray let out a growling huff. "Guilt and pity are wafting off you so strongly I'm practically strangling on them. Blakely, what happened to me is not your fault. Nor is it your responsibility to atone for anything."

"Is that what you think? That I'm atoning for some self-assessed sin?"

"Isn't it?"

God, the man was infuriating and a major pain in her ass sometimes.

"No. I'm fully aware the only ones truly responsible for what happened to you are the people involved in framing you—your mother, her boyfriend and your sister."

Gray flinched, which made her regret the words, even if they were the truth.

"We started something. I won't abandon you or what we're doing simply because we got a few of the answers. Especially not when those answers raised more questions."

"Maybe I don't want your help anymore."

It was Blakely's turn to flinch. His words hit her straight in the chest, bruising her just as much as any real punch could have.

"Is that true?"

"Hell, no. I never could have gotten this far without you."

"So why are you trying to push me away?"

Gray closed his eyes. With a groan, he sank back into the chair. "Because you scare the hell out of me."

The confession was just as startling as anything else he'd said to her. "*I* scare you? That's impossible. I'm no one with no significance."

This time, when Gray looked at her with anger in his eyes, the emotion was clearly directed straight at her. "Don't ever say that again. Yes, you scare me. I've truly known you for a little over a week and in that time, you've become the most important person in my life. But my life is utter crap at the moment and I really don't want to drag anyone else into it, least of all someone I actually like and am starting to care a great deal for."

Blakely's mouth opened and closed. Words formed in her head, but wouldn't tumble out. Until she finally said, "Oh."

"Yeah, oh."

What the heck was she supposed to do with that?

"I'm past starting to care a great deal for you, Gray. And you've quickly become the most important person in my life, too."

Apparently, she was going to be more honest with him than she'd meant to. Suddenly, a wave of heat washed over her body. What was she doing? Uneasiness filled her, not because she didn't mean what she'd said, but because the truth of her words made her vulnerable in a way she'd never let herself become before.

Relationships had never been her strength. In fact, she'd been accused of being cold and reserved by more than one boyfriend. And, no doubt, they'd all been right. Her father had taught her not to trust, a lesson that had been damn hard to unlearn.

Even now, the thought of letting Gray that close, letting him become important to her, had alarm bells going off inside her head. She was stupid for even considering it, wasn't she?

A week ago, she would have convinced herself that the fact he was a criminal meant he couldn't be trusted…but knowing what she did now, that felt like a cop-out.

But it also didn't make it any easier to let down those protective walls.

"You should take the opportunity I'm giving you and walk away."

Every self-preservation instinct inside her was screaming to do exactly as he suggested. But she couldn't make herself do it.

She didn't want to.

"No."

In the end, uttering that single word was the easiest decision she'd ever made.

Eleven

Gray couldn't decide if Blakely's decision was stupid or noble. Maybe a little of both. She should walk away. There was no doubt in his mind that would be the smartest thing for both of them.

A jumble of conflicting emotions churned in Gray's belly. Anger, frustration, hurt, apprehension. He couldn't shake the feeling of waiting for the other shoe to drop.

And that fear didn't dissipate two days later, when Joker gave them a rundown of what he'd uncovered about his sister.

"You said Kinley, your sister, was sixteen when she ran off on her own?"

Gray, Joker, Blakely, Stone and Finn all sat around the conference table at Stone Surveillance. Everyone who'd been instrumental in getting Gray to this point was there with him.

Why did it feel so monumental? Like another crossroads in his life. An unexpected one.

"That's what my birth mother said."

"I still can't believe you have a sister you never knew about," Stone grumbled. "This is an utter cluster, man. I'm so sorry."

That was Stone, apologizing for something that wasn't his fault. Taking the weight of the world onto his shoulders.

Finn, on the other hand, drawled, "Look on the bright side. At least this sister hasn't disowned you."

Gray laughed. He had to. "No, but she framed me for embezzlement."

"By accident."

So his mother said, but he wasn't convinced.

Joker chimed in, like he could read Gray's mind. "I wouldn't be so positive."

His stomach tightened, the muscles knotting into a tangle it felt like no one would be able to unravel. "Tell me."

Opening a dossier, Joker spread a bunch of papers across the table.

Blakely immediately jumped up, pulling several of them closer for inspection. Gray let her look. But he wasn't entirely certain he was ready to know what they contained.

"This chick is amazing," Joker said. "Who did you say trained her?"

"I didn't." Mostly because he had no clue beyond

what his mother had shared. "My mother said she'd shown a natural aptitude at an early age and her father started teaching her."

"That makes sense. Sure, there are some young IT geniuses who could figure this stuff out on their own, but she's really damn slick for someone so young."

It hadn't taken Gray long to do the math. His sister was now twenty-four, give or take a few months. He didn't even know when her birthday was. And that made his stomach tighten even more.

Growing up, he'd desperately wanted someone in his life he could be close to. His father hadn't given a damn about him, unless he could be useful in some way. His father had been too wrapped up in his business affairs. And his mother had been happy to leave Gray's upbringing to anyone else she could pay to fulfill the role.

Maybe that was the problem. He'd gained a sister only to immediately lose her because she'd been instrumental in the worst moments of his life. Karma really was a bitch, although he still wasn't sure what he'd ever done to deserve her disdain.

"Yeah, yeah, she's brilliant. We get it," Finn groused. "Could you hurry this up? I've got things to do and places to break into."

Gray rolled his eyes. Trust Finn to be in a hurry for a little B&E. Luckily, these days his extracurricular activities were wholly sanctioned. Not to mention profitable for their business.

"No, man. I don't think you understand. I've never met another hacker that I couldn't track within a few hours. Everyone leaves a trail, even if they don't mean to. Bread crumbs are easy to follow when you know what to look for. This girl…" Joker looked chagrined. "She's the best. Better than me."

Shit. Gray sat up in his chair. *Joker* was the best he'd ever seen, which was why Gray had cultivated the relationship and convinced the man to work for Stone Surveillance. Joker had single-handedly uncovered information that had been instrumental in saving Piper's life and exonerating Finn from being set up by his wife's grandfather.

"Does that mean you can't find her?"

Joker glared at him. "Of course not. It just means it took me longer than I would have liked. But like I said, everyone leaves bread crumbs…even if they think they're sweeping them all up."

Gray sank into his chair. The comforting weight of Blakely's hand landed on the curve of his thigh. She squeezed, silently giving him her support. He hadn't realized how much he'd needed it until that moment.

Setting his hand over hers, he squeezed back, a silent thank-you.

"It took a while, but I traced her trail backward for the past eight years, right after she left Vegas. Most of that time, she bounced from place to place across the world. A few months in Paris, a couple in Thailand, Venezuela, Brazil, South Africa, Iceland. There was no rhyme or reason, at least none I could figure out."

He was damn good with patterns, so Gray would hazard a guess that if Joker couldn't find one, there probably wasn't one.

"She never stayed long in any place and she rarely came back to the States. She was here during your trial, though. One of her longer periods in one place, actually."

"Here, as in Charleston?"

Joker nodded.

"Why the heck would she be here?" It made no sense. They knew she was responsible for framing him. They also knew she'd stolen another twenty million. Why put herself in jeopardy by coming so close to his trial?

"To make sure it went as she wanted?" Stone mused.

"Or maybe because she felt guilty about what happened," Blakely countered, her eyebrows pulled down into a sharp V of irritation.

"We can speculate all day, but there's no way to know for sure. I think we can all agree it's suspect." At least, that was Gray's take on it. No matter what his sister's motives for coming to Charleston back then…they obviously hadn't been to see he didn't pay for a crime he didn't commit.

"It gets weirder," Joker said.

"Weirder?" Finn's dark eyebrows winged up.

"Once I was able to track her movements, it didn't take me long to uncover several accounts in her name."

"Let me guess—the balance started out at twenty million?"

Joker's mouth twisted into a wry grimace. "Yep."

"How much is left?"

"Just over thirty million."

"Excuse me?"

"And that's in one account."

A sly grin stretched across Finn's lips. "The little minx really is a genius. She's managed to evade everyone and grow her money."

"Oh, she's done more than that."

For the first time since they'd sat down, Gray realized Joker's voice was tinged with respect and pride each time he talked about her. The rascal was impressed.

"Explain."

"Kinley hasn't just been investing your money for the past eight years. She used a little, but each time would eventually replace it with interest."

"And how has she accomplished this?" Stone, who'd been silent and observant much of the time finally asked.

"By stealing money from other people."

Why didn't that surprise him? "Why haven't we heard about these thefts? Did she decide to change her tactics and go after smaller amounts to fly under the radar?"

"Actually, it's the opposite. Your twenty million is small change. She's managed to steal almost a billion dollars from various people."

"Now I'm less impressed that her bank account has thirty million in it," Finn quipped.

"That's because she doesn't keep the money. Or doesn't keep most of it. She has another account with a few million in it that she appears to use when she needs to disappear again."

"So what's she doing with the rest of the money?"

"Giving it to various charitable organizations."

"Say that again."

"You heard me."

"She's stolen a billion dollars to give it all away?" Finn's incredulity wasn't surprising. The only thing keeping him on the straight and narrow was Genevieve. Without her, Gray's friend would be just as crooked as his sister might be.

"Not only that, but she's managed to keep the thefts out of the media because she's targeted people who can't afford to report the crimes."

"Because the money is dirty."

"Exactly. She's targeted some of the biggest crime syndicates in the world—Russian, Chinese, American, Central and South American. If the money came from human trafficking, selling drugs or trading in weapons, she's taken it."

No wonder Joker was verging on idolizing his sister.

"Let me see if I'm getting this right. My sister, a genius hacker, disappeared eight years ago after framing me for embezzling money from my family's company. She took that money, placed it in an account and hasn't touched it the entire time."

"No, she's touched it, but she treats it like a loan and always pays it back. With interest."

Right, because most criminals worried about interest when they committed a crime like stealing.

"She's spent those eight years targeting and stealing money from criminals around the world and donating the proceeds to charities."

"Most of it. She keeps some money, but not a lot. Not nearly as much as she could. And almost in every instance, the money she does keep funds the next target."

Gray stared at Joker, not really seeing him. Part of him had expected this endeavor would uncover things he might not want to know. Being targeted as a patsy for embezzlement didn't normally happen to people with squeaky clean lives. And he'd hardly been a saint.

But never in a million years had he expected to discover he'd been living a lie and his mother wasn't really his. Or that he had a sister. Who'd framed him, but now operated as the Robin Hood of hackers.

Honestly, he had no idea what to do with this information or how to feel about it all. The hits just kept coming. Like he'd been in the worst fight of his life and was losing, something he wasn't used to and didn't particularly like.

"Where is she now?" Blakely's soft voice filled the silence at the table, asking the question he was too numb to ask.

"Bali. She's been there ever since you were released. It's the longest she's stayed in one place since Vegas."

Gray was too stunned to wonder what that was supposed to mean.

"But there's more."

He wasn't certain he could handle more right now. "She's been watching you."

That got Stone's attention. Before Gray could even react, his friend's elbows were on the table and he was leaning hard toward Joker. "What do you mean she's been watching him?"

"She has a back door into all of his electronics. She's been monitoring his email and internet traffic. My guess is she's also been listening in and watching through those same devices."

Which explained why Joker had told them to leave their cell phones and electronic devices outside before coming into the conference room. Gray had initially chalked it up to his friend's paranoia.

"You could have told us."

"I wanted to explain before you jumped to conclusions."

"What conclusions would those be? That my sister has been tracking my every movement since I got out of prison? For what purpose? To frame me again? Steal from me again?"

Blakely's hand moved to his arm, tugging. He hadn't realized he'd stood up until he looked down and discovered she was looking up. Slowly, Gray let his legs fold beneath him and he sat back down into his chair.

"I really don't think that's it, man. I think she's been saving the money and is trying to figure out how to give it back to you."

Wonderful. His sister had grown a conscience and was spying on him so she could make amends.

"Why didn't she just send a certified check?" Gray could hear the petty sarcasm in his voice, but couldn't stop it. He was pissed and she was the easiest target right now. Even if his brain told him she might not deserve it.

"Gray," Blakely said, her voice calm and soothing. "That's not going to accomplish anything."

Of course it wouldn't, but it had felt good. At least for a second.

But that feeling was fleeting. Logic, that's what he needed right now. And he knew just who would give it to him.

Turning, he focused squarely on Blakely. "What now?"

Her lips turned up at the corners into a sad, understanding smile that somehow managed to start unknotting the ropes in his belly.

"We go find her. I have a feeling she's waiting for you."

Was she? Gray wasn't sure he was ready for that encounter. But Blakely was right. It's what he needed to do.

This plane ride was much different from the last one. The flight was longer, but it hadn't felt that way.

The moment they soared into the air, Gray unbuckled his seat belt. Reaching across her, he did the same for hers. The metal edges clanged loudly against the seat as they dropped open.

"What are you doing?"

"Taking advantage of the time we have."

Grasping her hands, Gray urged her out of her seat and into the narrow aisle. He led them toward the back of the plane, past a small galley and through a doorway that she'd missed the first time they were on board.

Stepping into the room tucked away, Blakely thought, *Of course it has a full bedroom.*

Gray tugged her inside. And immediately found her mouth with his. The kiss was explosive, going from nothing to red-hot in mere seconds. It was easy to let herself sink into the craving that was always present when he touched her. But tonight, Gray seemed to need more.

Pulling back, he looked down at her, his ever-green eyes filled with passion, but something stronger. Something softer and more enduring.

Something that had hope and uneasiness twisting in her gut.

Slowly, he led her over to the bed. Without saying a word, Gray reached for the hem of her shirt and pulled it up and over. The rest of her clothes quickly followed until she was standing before him entirely naked.

Any other time, she would have felt vulnerable, but not now. Not with a look of such awe and need stamped across his face.

She needed to touch him. To feel him. Now.

Blakely quickly added his clothes to the pile at their feet. An arm wrapped around her back, and Gray urged her to the bed. The coverlet beneath her skin was soft and cool, inviting. But that thought lasted a nanosecond before the blazing heat of his body joined hers.

The drag and pull of his skin against hers made Blakely arch up, searching for more. Always more with him. She could never get enough.

His mouth found her, raining kisses across her entire body. He lingered here and there, nipping and laving, worshipping and teasing. Blakely did the same, letting her mouth and hands explore him with a languid urgency that was both breathtaking and compelling.

Words were unnecessary, but he whispered them, anyway. How beautiful she was. What he planned to do to her body. How he intended to make her writhe with desire, pleasure and passion.

And he was true to each promise.

Blakely's breath caught in her lungs, almost as if her body was too busy with other things to remember that basic function. She wanted to make his body hum with the same rich energy that he was building inside her.

Finding the long, hard length of him nestled between them, she wrapped her hand around the hard shaft and tugged. He growled, the vibration of the sound rumbling through her own body.

Rolling them both, Blakely positioned herself above him and used her hold to guide him home. A sigh of satisfaction and relief left her parted lips. Blakely threw back her head, relishing the joy of feeling him buried deep inside her.

But after a few moments, that wasn't enough.

She began to ride him, rolling her hips back and forth in an effort to get more. Gray's hands gripped her hips, guiding her, moving her, faster and faster until the world began to turn black around the edges.

Blakely's breath panted in and out. Her body burned, heat and need building higher and higher.

One moment she was upright, the next her back was bouncing off the mattress as Gray pounded in and out of her.

Somehow, as he'd flipped them both, he'd managed to find her hands. Twining their fingers together, he used the hold to keep her steady. His mouth found hers, the kiss as deep as the connection between them.

The orgasm exploded through Blakely. Gray's bark of relief was right behind as he thrust deep, once, twice, three more times, before collapsing onto the bed beside her.

Their limbs tangled, bodies sweaty and replete.

After several seconds, Blakely leaned up and stared down into his gorgeous face. His eyes were open, a self-satisfied smile stretching his lips as he watched her.

"Well, isn't it quite handy to have a bed at thirty thousand feet?"

Twelve

Blakely lounged against the pile of pillows. They should probably get up and get dressed, but she wasn't motivated to move, not after the multiple orgasms Gray had just given her. Honestly, she wasn't certain her legs would hold her, anyway, if she tried.

Gray didn't appear to be in too much of a hurry to go back to their seats, either. And she had to admit the view wasn't hard to look at.

He was sprawled across the bed, sheets tangled between his thighs, completely uncaring. Half of his delectable ass was on display. Blakely was tempted to tug at the covers just so she could see the rest. But she knew if she did, they'd end up having sex again, and as much as she enjoyed sex with Gray, her body needed a few more minutes of recovery.

Gray's fingers played across her skin, tracing mindless patterns over her hips, belly and ribs. He had her tucked beneath him, his head resting on the curve of her waist. He was quiet and a little pensive, just as he'd been earlier when they first boarded the plane.

Threading her fingers into his hair, Blakely gently pulled until his eyes found hers. "Hey, everything's going to be okay."

"I know." His words said one thing, but the darkness lurking in his gaze suggested another.

"You've been hit by so much in the past several years, Gray. I really hope this is the start to everything changing. Your sister could help prove your innocence."

"Sure, but only by admitting to a crime herself."

There was a fly in the ointment for sure. As much as she liked to be able to think most humans were honorable enough to admit to a crime in order to save someone else from paying the price...she knew first-hand that wasn't likely. Most people were selfish and could only see the impact something like that would make on their own lives.

What struck her as surprising was that a few weeks ago she wouldn't have considered it possible at all. But Gray... He was starting to make her feel like there were good people still left in the world.

Maybe his sister would be one of them.

"Why do you think she's been watching you?"

"No idea."

"But you have a theory."

A frown crinkled the corners of his gorgeous green eyes. "Yes."

Blakely smoothed his hair away from his forehead so she could see him better, waiting.

"I'd like to think her guilty conscience means she's been trying to figure out how to fix what she screwed up. But the rest of me…"

Blakely's stomach dropped right along with Gray's voice.

"I keep thinking she's had plenty of time to act if she wanted to. However, if she's been waiting for another opportunity to take from me? To ruin my life some more?"

Blakely shook her head. Something deep inside told her that wasn't what his sister wanted. Maybe she was being naive—a state she'd never been afflicted by before—but it didn't add up.

"To what purpose? You don't have access to the company anymore. Sure, you have plenty of money of your own, but we both know she could have taken that at any point."

"True."

"And the people she's been stealing from have been terrible human beings."

"I'm a convicted felon."

Frustration tinged Blakely's voice. "Because she *framed* you."

Gray's gaze dropped back down to stare at a spot on the bed. He continued to trace patterns on her skin. Goose bumps spread over her arms and legs, but she ignored them.

"You know, going to prison saved my life."

Blakely's own fingers traced across his shoulders, paying special attention to the puckered skin under the ridge of his shoulder blade. She hadn't asked, but assumed he'd gotten the scar during his time inside. He'd told her he'd gotten several others that way.

She couldn't understand how anyone could feel a situation that had left multiple marks across his body had saved him.

"How?"

His mouth twisted into a wry grimace. "I was aimless and spoiled before I went inside."

Blakely couldn't dispute that statement, because it was clearly true.

"I spent my entire life being given everything. I never had to earn anything, not truly. Inside, I had to earn everything. But the most important thing I learned how to earn was respect. Respect for myself and respect from others."

Blakely's stomach clenched. She wanted to wrap her arms around him and hold him close, but something told her this wasn't the time.

"Don't get me wrong, at first I was pissed. Angry at everyone and everything. I was still entitled, wearing the idea that life had treated me unfairly like a chip on my shoulder."

She was surprised he wasn't still pissed. He'd lost seven years of his life because someone else had screwed him over. And no matter how hard she tried, Blakely couldn't forget the role she'd played in putting him there, either.

"But then I met Stone and Finn. Separately, we were vulnerable to the other gangs and groups that formed inside. But together, we had power and quickly discovered how to demand deference from the other inmates.

"The experience stripped away my entitled lifestyle and made me realize I didn't like the person I'd been very much."

That must have been a difficult moment. Not many people had the fortitude to truly evaluate themselves and admit they weren't proud of who they'd become.

"That takes real strength, Gray."

He huffed out a reluctant laugh. "I don't know about that. But it definitely wasn't a comfortable experience. Stone helped me, though. He's one of the most honest men I've ever met."

Blakely could see that. She'd only had a few dealings with him so far, but he'd seemed very fair and concerned for her comfort and safety.

"It wasn't an easy process. There are things about my time inside I'll never tell anyone, because I'm not proud of them, but also because unless you've been there you can't understand."

Her fingers traced the white, puckered flesh again. Part of her wanted him to be able to share anything with her, but she understood. There were things about her past—her childhood—that she had no intention of sharing with anyone, including Gray.

At the end of the day, the details didn't matter, anyway. What did were the lessons and growth that had come from them.

"It didn't take Stone, Finn or me long to realize in order to stay on the right side of the other inmates, as well as the guards, we needed something that both sides wanted. Inside, boredom is a serious problem. Hours and hours of idleness is a breeding ground for serious issues."

She could absolutely understand how that would be true.

"We ended up running an underground fighting ring. A perfect solution for everyone. Stone managed and arranged things. He handled the details and ensured the guards' buy-in."

"So, basically, he worked the connections and people?" It was the role Stone appeared to fill for Stone Surveillance, as well. He was the face of the company.

"Exactly. Finn handled the books, worked the betting pools and ran the numbers. He also used his charm and personality to stoke friendly rivalries and build hype for whatever fight was coming up."

Blakely had a feeling she knew the answer to her question, but she had to ask it, anyway…even if a huge part of her didn't necessarily want the answer. "And what did you do?"

Gray's mouth twisted into a self-deprecating smile. "I fought."

Of course he had. Blakely's stomach clenched uncomfortably. A spurt of fear shot into her system, as if he was preparing for a fight now.

"I'd never been in a fight before walking into that prison. I was too soft. I'd always used money and status to get myself out of any difficult situations."

180 THE SINNER'S SECRET

"So why did you take on that role? Why couldn't you have been the bookie and let Finn fight?"

Gray's burst of laughter tickled across her skin. "Yeah, right. Finn is a lot of things, but he's too soft to fight. Besides, his dexterous hands are a valuable commodity."

Blakely's eyes rolled. Sure they were. He'd been a jewel thief.

"I was good at it. The training gave me something to focus on outside of my feelings of anger and injustice. I discovered discipline. I finally had to work for something…or risk getting my ass beaten."

"How often did that happen?"

His lips twitched. "A few times in the beginning. By the end…no one could beat me."

Blakely wasn't surprised. Gray might be many things, but the man she knew was driven and determined.

"I learned a lot about myself in the process. But most of all, I grew into a man I could be proud of."

Blakely shifted, using her leverage to roll them both. He dropped onto the bed, his large body sprawling. Blakely's hips settled over his, their legs tangling together.

The hard ridge of his sex stirred between them, making her own sex pulse with a reminder and demand.

But there was something she wanted to say first.

Wrapping her hands around the base of his skull, Blakely brought her face close to his, making sure she filled his entire gaze.

"You are one of the best men I've ever known, Gray Lockwood. You're honorable, strong, quiet and resourceful. I hate that you went through a terrible time in your life to become the man you are, but the man you are is amazing."

His eyes sharpened, going hot and hard.

His fingers buried deep into her hair, holding her steady as he surged up and found her mouth.

Apparently, words weren't necessary anymore.

They landed in Kuta. Gray was certain the city was gorgeous—they were in Bali, after all. Surprisingly enough, in all his travels during his younger years, Bali had never made it onto the list. Perhaps because he'd been more interested in wild adventures than calming, peaceful vistas.

Unfortunately, the view was still lost on him since his mind wasn't on taking in the sights. Apparently, neither was Blakely's, which shouldn't have surprised him, but did.

She was efficient and focused as they followed the man who greeted them as they disembarked the plane. Striding before him across the tarmac, *that* was the sight Gray couldn't tear his gaze away from. The compact, lithe movements of her body. The lush, rounded globe of her ass hugged by well-worn denim. Hell, he hadn't even realized Blakely owned a pair of jeans until she'd pulled them on when they'd finally decided to climb from the bed.

He liked seeing her relaxed and casual. Something told him not many people got to experience that side of her. He tried not to convince himself it was important she felt comfortable enough to let him in... but it was.

They reached a dark green Jeep, clearly set up for off-roading adventures. The top and doors were off, roll bars showing. Several men who'd followed behind with their luggage quickly stowed everything in the back. Blakely didn't hesitate, but grasped one of the bars and boosted herself up into the lifted vehicle.

Reaching into her bag, she rummaged around until she found a hair band and quickly pulled it into a knot at the base of her skull. Shaking his head, Gray followed her. Beneath his breath he murmured, "Always prepared."

"What?" Blakely turned to him, her eyebrows beetled together in confusion.

"Nothing."

But that was Blakely to a *T*. She hadn't questioned or hesitated. She'd simply seen the vehicle they were taking and adjusted accordingly. It never would have entered her mind to complain and request something else. There had been plenty of women in his life—before—that would have stood outside the Jeep and pitched a fit, refusing to get in because it would mess up their hair.

Climbing up, Gray settled into his seat. Reaching over, he grasped Blakely's hand and pulled it into his own lap. He simply needed to touch her right now.

The drive across the island was beautiful. But the closer they got to the villa he'd rented, the more his stomach churned. After some digging, Joker had finally been able to send him an address. His sister had apparently rented a small place on the beach not far from where they were staying.

In less than an hour he might be confronting the person responsible for his imprisonment. And she was his half sister.

Was he ready for this?

They pulled up at the villa. It was gorgeous, but Gray didn't particularly care. He was used to staying in beautiful places. Often took it for granted.

Blakely didn't.

She hopped out of the Jeep, her feet hitting the ground with an audible thud. And she simply stood there, staring at the place.

It took several moments for her reaction to catch Gray's attention. But when it did, he decided then and there they were coming back to Bali the first chance they got. He wanted to put that look of wonder and surprise on her face every chance he could.

After handing off a bag to the staff that had come out to meet them, Gray walked over to her. Wrapping his arms around her, he pulled Blakely against his body. She willingly went, leaning into him without hesitation.

"It's beautiful."

"Wait until you see the view from the bedroom." The master suite opened out to the pool, which overlooked a stretch of private beach. They could lie in bed and watch the sunset…and sunrise.

Twisting around, she looked up at him. "You didn't

have to get a whole villa, Gray. It's just the two of us. Surely they have hotel rooms on the island."

"Of course, but I thought we might want privacy."

Her gaze sharpened. "Because you intend to make me scream your name repeatedly or because you expect things to go badly with your sister?"

Gray huffed out a laugh. "Both."

A smile teased the corners of her lips. "I'm in for the first and I'm going to hope the second doesn't happen."

Gray was going to, as well, but he wasn't holding his breath. Nothing added up where his sister was concerned, so he really had no way of making an educated guess as to how this encounter was going to go.

He was about to say as much when the cell in his pocket buzzed. Pulling it out, he glanced at the number on the screen. His belly tightened, but he answered the call, anyway.

"Joker."

"She's there right now, but she's not planning to stay long. She started moving money a couple of hours ago. Looks like she's getting ready to run."

Because she'd figured out they were close?

Gray had purposely left all of his electronics back in Charleston, including his personal cell. This one was a Stone Surveillance burner he'd grabbed on their way out of town. Not only had he needed to evade his sister's scrutiny, but he was also still on probation technically, and not allowed to leave the country without approval.

"How did she figure out we're here?"

Joker grumbled something unintelligible, but clearly he wasn't happy. Finally, he said, "She didn't. Someone else found her."

Gray let out an expletive. Shitty timing. "Who?"

"A Russian mob boss she screwed over about two years ago."

Perfect. "It going to be a problem?"

"Not if you get to her first."

Grabbing Blakely's hand, he started pulling her back to the Jeep. Whistling to get the attention of their driver, Gray pointed at the Jeep. The guy nodded, then passed off the piece of luggage he'd been carrying. Jogging over, he launched his small frame into the driver's seat.

Gray didn't wait for Blakely to pause, but grabbed her around the waist and boosted her up into the Jeep. Rounding the vehicle, he showed their driver the address before following.

He'd expected to have a little time to prepare for this encounter. But maybe this was better.

Thirteen

Blakely was patient and simply went along for the ride. He hadn't even bothered to tell her what was going on until they were already speeding away from their villa. The whole time Gray's mind raced with what would happen if the Russian muscle arrived first, anxiety gripping his gut.

No one deserved that.

The drive up to his sister's place was severely different from the drive up to theirs. Wild vegetation obscured the view of the house, not just from the road, but from the long, winding drive. Their rental had been meticulously landscaped—the lush vegetation had been tamed to give a sense of tropical decadence.

The house itself was also much different. Small and old, clearly it had seen better days. Their villa screamed affluence and attention, not because Gray cared about stuff like that, but because he could afford the comforts it provided.

His sister could afford the same things. But something told him she'd chosen this place on purpose. Not only because it was well hidden, but also in order to not draw any undue attention.

Before they actually reached the house, Gray leaned forward and tapped their driver on the shoulder, telling him to stop. She might have already heard the Jeep, but in case she hadn't, he didn't want to spook her.

Jumping down, he walked around to help Blakely from the vehicle. Grasping her hand, they quietly walked the rest of the path up to the house.

It was silent and dark. No lights on inside, which made a tight band constrict Gray's chest. Were they too late? Had they missed her?

Rather than knock, he tried the knob, but wasn't surprised to find it locked. No one who made a habit of screwing over powerful people left the front door unlocked. Not if they were smart, and from everything he'd learned, his sister was extremely intelligent.

He could pick the lock, a little skill Finn had shared. But his friend had also imparted another piece of wisdom—don't make a simple job harder than it has to be.

Urging Blakely to follow behind him, Gray circled the house. It might not have much to offer in the way of luxury, but the view was breathtaking. Like most villas here, the back of the house had a huge out-door area. The living space was open to the breezy outdoor sitting area and a path straight down to the water. There were doors that could be closed for se-curity, but right now they were standing wide open.

Which told him that either his sister had left in a hurry, not bothering to secure the place, or she might be somewhere inside.

Taking a chance, Gray stepped up onto the back deck and raised his voice. "Kinley."

Her name reverberated against the terra-cotta tiles. His instincts hummed. A sound echoed from deep in-side the darkened house. A muffled curse.

"Kinley, I'm not here to hurt you. I'm just here to talk."

Slowly, his eyes adjusted to the dark. Moonlight high above washed everything with a ghostly silver gray. He inched forward. And a soft voice floated into the darkness. "Stop."

Blakely's hand clamped down on his arm. Slowly, Kinley materialized out of the shadows as she moved forward into the watery light. "Don't come any closer."

Gray held up his open hands in the universal sign that he meant no harm. "I'm not here to hurt you."

"That's a lie. Why wouldn't you be here to hurt me? I ruined your life."

"You know who I am."

"Of course I know who you are."

Gray took a deep breath, pulling in air and hold-ing it for several seconds before slowly letting it out on a warm stream. Some of the tension that had been tightening his shoulders flowed out with it.

"All I want is to talk."

"Bullshit. You want to make me pay for what I did to you."

Gray tilted his head sideways, really studying his sister. She didn't look a thing like their mother, but that didn't mean she wasn't just as beautiful. In fact, she was even more striking. Her inky hair hung in long, thick curls down her back, contrasting with her creamy skin, making it glow in the moonlight. He couldn't tell their exact color, but her eyes were dark, as well—probably brown. She was tall—he'd guess only a few inches short of six feet. But her body was lean, a runner's build.

Gray wasn't sure what he'd expected, but it wasn't this beautiful, strong woman standing before him. Maybe he'd expected a child. The sixteen-year-old teenager who had influenced his life. Kinley was hardly that. Gray knew within seconds that she was fully capable of taking care of herself. Because she'd had to do it for the last eight years…or even longer than that.

In that moment, Gray realized they had much more in common than a shared parent.

"I want to understand what happened. Yes, I have questions. But I don't want you to pay for anything. I know you were only sixteen when our mother convinced you to steal that money."

Kinley took several steps closer, coming even farther into the light. "Wait, what?" Her dark eyebrows winged down into a deep V of confusion. "*Our* mother?"

Oh, hell. She didn't know.

Gray's mouth opened and closed. Of course Cece had never told Kinley. Why would she?

The job had been about his father, not about him. Kinley had accidentally framed him, pulling him into the mess. Without that mistake, none of it would have touched him, so there'd been no reason to tell his sister that he existed.

Blakely's soft hand landed on his shoulder. She squeezed and then took over when he wasn't sure he had the words to continue.

"Gray is your half brother. Your mother was angry with his father for refusing to give her more money. That's why she had you steal from Lockwood Industries. You were supposed to frame his father for embezzlement, but you put the money in Gray's accounts instead."

Kinley stared at the woman who'd just rocked her world, dumbfounded by the unexpected revelation. Her gaze jerked to Gray Lockwood, a man who had become as familiar to her as her own reflection. Hell, she'd spent hours watching him over the last several months. A lot more time than the cursory glances she'd taken in the mirror.

How had she missed it?

She'd dug into this guy's background. Read every piece of documentation she could find about his life. She knew he'd been a math whiz as a kid, but hated history. She knew he'd had his appendix out when he was eleven. She even knew the brand of underwear he preferred to buy.

"Not possible."

That was the only conclusion she could come up with. There would have been some paper trail. Some indication.

"I assure you, it's not only possible, it's the truth. My father had an affair with your mother. She got pregnant. My mother couldn't conceive so he paid Cece to give up the baby. My birth certificate was falsified."

Kinley let out a sharp laugh. "Money can buy anything, huh?"

"Something like that."

She stared at him. He was handsome and a little scary. Gray Lockwood reminded her of the men currently chasing after her. Despite the silver-spoon upbringing, he still carried an edge of danger that nothing could hide. He was big and broad and clearly possessed the skills to protect himself if push came to shove.

"Why should I believe you?"

Gray shrugged. "You don't have to. Yet. I'm happy to get the tests to prove we're siblings…after we get you out of here. We have reason to believe the Russians after you will be here in less than twenty minutes."

Kinley swore under her breath. She'd always known her choices would catch up to her sooner or later. *You piss off enough powerful, vindictive people and eventually you pay the price.*

And she'd been okay with that. In theory. Now that the reality was breathing hot and heavy down her neck...

She'd done a lot of good for a lot of people. She'd righted a lot of wrongs. That was going to have to be good enough. The reality was, there was no one in her life who would give a damn if she disappeared. The Russians could kill her and her death wouldn't be a blip on a single radar.

Which was the life she'd chosen.

But she wasn't ready to give up just yet.

Spinning on her heel, Kinley headed back into the darkened house. She entered the room she'd set up as an office months ago, when she'd settled in Bali. She'd picked the house for very specific reasons, one of which was that despite the run-down appearance and out-of-the-way location, the house was wired like a high-tech ops center. Or at least it was now.

She started placing stuff into the open cases she'd abandoned when Gray had tripped her silent alarm. Most of her computers, servers, racks and equipment were already put away. She only had a few more, and packing them wouldn't take her five minutes. The issue would be getting everything loaded into her car in time.

Next time, she was going to invest in a heavy-duty cart so she didn't have to lug the awkward cases one at a time.

Her brother—she still wasn't ready to accept

that—and the woman appeared. They stood in the doorway just watching, without saying anything. Clearly, they weren't there to hurt her, but the Russians would, so that danger was more pressing.

She'd deal with her brother and the woman later. Or not.

Grabbing the first box, Kinley tried to keep in the groan of effort, but couldn't quite make it.

Her brother shot forward, snatching it from her before she could protest. Lifting it like it was nothing, he spun on his heel and headed out the front door. Kinley started to chase after him—he was holding some damn expensive equipment and she really didn't want him to disappear with it.

But she stopped. There was no way she was going to win if they ended up in a wrestling match. Better to grab another box and get it into her car. She had the money to replace anything he took, even if it would be a huge pain in the ass.

Battles and wars and all that. She was picking and choosing.

Kinley headed out behind him, cognizant that the woman who'd come in with Gray had also grabbed one of the boxes stacked in the corner and was following. Great.

Ahead of her, her brother approached a Jeep idling in front of the house. He didn't pause, but lifted up the box and put it into the back. He motioned for her to do the same, but she was in no mood to comply. Instead, she started over to the small SUV she'd bought for ten thousand dollars when she'd arrived to the island.

The woman continued past her and dropped her box into the Jeep before silently returning back to the house for more.

Dammit.

It wasn't worth the breath to argue or try to stop them.

Instead, Kinley popped the door on her car and set the case inside. Gray came behind her and immediately pulled it back out again, then carried it over to the Jeep.

Fed up, she finally turned, put her hands on his back and shoved hard. "What do you think you're doing? Leave my shit alone!"

"Kinley, I'm not letting you deal with the Russians by yourself. Let us help you get out of here. I have a private jet at the airport waiting on standby to take us wherever you want."

Why the hell would he do that?

Kinley stared at the man in front of her, completely dumbfounded. "I ruined your life."

"No, you didn't, but we can talk about that later. Right now, we need to get out of here."

The woman came back with another case and stacked it on the others. Anger, fear, desperation and hope all mixed together in her belly, making her want to throw up. The two of them were certainly acting like they wanted to help.

The faint sound of an engine lifted into the air.

"Shit," Gray said. "They're here. Get in."

"But I don't have everything."

"There's no more time." Grasping her arm, Gray

pulled her over to the Jeep, gripped her waist and tossed her into the back seat. The woman with him scrambled up into the other side as Gray vaulted into the passenger seat.

The driver, clearly a local, spun the tires as Gray urged, "Hurry up."

One of the other reasons she'd chosen the house was because there were two paths in and out, something the driver clearly already knew because he headed in the opposite direction of the approaching car.

Everyone was silent as they jolted into the overgrown vegetation. Anxiety filled the air between them and they all waited to see if the car behind them would stop at the house or follow.

Kinley twisted so she could see out the back. And let out a huge sigh of relief when the wide circle of headlights stopped, shining straight onto the house. A handful of men jumped out of the two vehicles, swarming up onto the front porch.

That was all she caught before they took a hairpin turn and the house completely disappeared from view.

Turning around, Kinley stared at the back of her brother's head. Her world had just gotten very surreal.

The woman beside her leaned forward, catching her attention. Holding out a hand, she said, "Hi, I'm Blakely. I work with your brother."

The Jeep was silent and rife with tension. Blakely wanted to do or say something to cut it, but nothing would help. Gray was only in the front seat, but for some reason he suddenly felt very far away.

Not once since they'd gotten in had he looked back at her. Or at Kinley, for that matter. Blakely's stomach knotted with apprehension and uncertainty.

They pulled into the private entrance at the airport, racing toward the jet sitting on the tarmac.

Several people milled around. A few were loading luggage and cargo. Clearly, Gray had instructed someone to pack their things and bring them. She hadn't even seen him send a text or make a call.

But that was Gray, silently taking care of the things that needed attention.

They pulled up close to the jet. Several men raced forward, pulled Kinley's cases from the back and rushing them toward the plane.

"Wait," his sister protested, reaching for one. "I'm not going."

The man gave her a look like she'd grown two heads, shook off her hold and then proceeded to do exactly as he'd been instructed.

Gray approached his sister. "Kinley, we'll take you wherever you want to go, but I can't leave you here while the Russians are so close. It's not safe."

Kinley shook her head. "Why are you doing this? Helping me?"

A small smile played at the edges of Gray's mouth. "I know about what you do. You steal money from really bad people and give it to those that need it."

"I stole money from *you*."

"Yes, you did. Did you mean to?"

Kinley threw her hands into the air. "Of course not!"

Gray shifted, rocking on his feet like he wanted to reach out to his sister, but stopped himself before actually touching her. "Trust me, my bank account is fine."

"I have the money. You can have it back. I've been trying to figure out how to put it into your accounts without screwing myself or you even worse than I already did."

"I know."

"You know?"

Gray took another step closer to his sister. "I happen to know a hacker who's almost as good as you are."

"Who?"

Gray's grin widened. "Not my info to share. But I have a feeling you'll have an opportunity to meet at some point."

Blakely watched Gray tentatively reach out a hand to Kinley and set it on her shoulder.

Brother and sister faced off, Kinley with a perplexed expression and Gray with hope. Blakely's chest tightened. It was a surreal moment, one she was grateful to witness.

Gray had lost so much. The only family he'd ever known abandoned him. He'd learned the woman who'd given birth to him never wanted him and didn't care what happened to him. Sure, he'd found two amazing friends that were as close as brothers, but at the end of the day it wasn't the same as blood.

God, she really hoped Gray was right and Kinley wouldn't screw him over, too. She was hopeful, but it was difficult for her not to let the cynicism of her childhood color that hope.

"I own a security company. We can always use someone with your skills."

"No." Kinley didn't even contemplate Gray's tentative offer. "I work alone."

"You still can. I'm just saying, if you ever want to freelance…" Gray pulled out a cell and handed it to her. "My number is programmed. Call me. Anytime."

"Just like that. You're going to let the twenty million dollars and everything else go?"

Gray shrugged. "It's not like I need it. Use it for something good, Kinley."

"You're not going to turn me in?"

Gray shook his head. "No."

Blakely took a step back. She wasn't surprised to hear him voice that decision, but it still made her heart hurt. He was giving up the one thing he'd been working so long and hard for.

Fourteen

Blakely had been quiet since they'd gotten onto the plane. A few hours ago, they'd made a fuel stop in Hong Kong. They'd also left Kinley there.

It had been difficult to watch his sister walk away. Not just because she was in danger, but because he'd just found her. And a huge part of him wanted the opportunity to get to know her better.

But that wasn't his choice. He'd made the offer of a position with Stone—from there it was up to her what happened next with her life. What he could control was what happened in his.

Gray watched the ground disappear beneath them as they rose higher into the sky. Soon enough, they'd be back in Charleston. He wasn't surprised when Blakely sat down in the chair next to his.

Since they'd boarded the plane, she'd been keeping a distance between them. Maybe she'd sensed he'd needed the space. Or maybe she was avoiding him.

He was so mentally and physically exhausted, at the moment he wasn't sure whether or not it mattered. The result was the same. There was this space between them that hadn't been there before.

"What now?"

Her question was simple. Unfortunately, the answer wasn't. Hell, he wasn't absolutely certain what she was really asking. But he could answer one thing.

"Nothing. We go back to the office and go on with life."

Leaning forward, Blakely put her elbows on her knees and dropped her head. "I was afraid you were going to say that. You're not going to tell the authorities or your father."

It wasn't a question. Clearly, she'd already figured out he wasn't. Not only had he said as much to Kinley, but deep down, he knew it was the right thing to do.

"It would put her in someone else's crosshairs and she's already got plenty of people chasing her."

"What about you?"

"What about me?"

"You deserve your life back, Gray. You didn't do anything wrong and you've lost everything."

Had he? Gray wasn't so sure that was true.

"Getting my life back would mean destroying hers." And he wasn't willing to do that. They might not have shared history, but they did share DNA. And at the end of the day, she was as much a victim in all of this as he was. He refused to punish her for her parents' manipulation and a mistake she'd made when she was sixteen.

"Not necessarily. She's really good at being a ghost. Just because you produce evidence that you were framed doesn't mean you need to give up her trail."

"Maybe, but it's a risk I'm not willing to take. My father has means and determination. At the moment, he thinks I have twenty million stashed somewhere. If he discovered someone else was in possession of those Lockwood assets...he'd stop at nothing to find the person responsible."

"Kinley's willing to give back the money."

"And that might help, but it won't stop him. I know him, and he's relentless when he's on a crusade. No, it's better if he never knows. I've already paid my debt to society, Blakely. I can't get those years back, no matter what."

"No, but you can get your family back. Your reputation and legacy."

Gray laughed, the sound bitter even to his own ears. "I don't really have a family, do I? And I never did. My father doesn't give a damn about me. He cares about appearances. The woman I thought was my mother couldn't care less what happens to me. And the mother who gave birth to me is only interested in what she can get out of me. No, thank you. I'm perfectly happy with the life I have."

"What life? Gray, I've spent the last few weeks with you. Your existence has been entirely wrapped up in proving your innocence. The last eight years. All I'm saying is, don't make this decision in haste."

A tight knot cramped Gray's stomach. Blakely stared at him through those pale blue eyes that always cut straight through him. He'd seen them filling with passion and heat. Hope and frustration. Right now, they were awash with guilt and disappointment.

"Don't give up the chance to clear your name. Everyone needs to know you're not a criminal. You deserve the chance to shake off that stigma."

In that moment, Gray realized just how important that was to her. Images of her father standing in the middle of the office hallway, everyone staring at the spectacle he'd created, flashed across his mind. Her embarrassment and irritation at the precinct. The tired disappointment in her voice as she'd talked about growing up with a criminal as a father.

Clearing his name had become a crusade for her, as well, and not simply because of the guilt she harbored for her part in putting him in jail.

Blakely had a clear sense of right and wrong thanks to the gray world her father lived in. She'd lived with the taint of that stigma her entire life, and she'd done everything she could to distance herself from it.

And if he didn't clear his name, being with him would taint her once again.

He couldn't ask her to do that. But he also couldn't use the information he had to clear his name.

"I'll think about it." Although he wouldn't. Standing up, Gray gave her a weak smile. "I'm going to make a few phone calls and take care of a few things back home." And he walked back into the bedroom.

This day was about to get worse, but just like the fights he'd been in, sometimes he just had to take a punch.

Gray had spent the rest of their flight in the bedroom, only coming back out minutes before they landed. Blakely almost regretted what she'd said, but she couldn't quite bring herself to get there. He'd worked so damn hard to prove his innocence, she hated to watch him walk away from the opportunity to get back everything he'd lost.

Maybe he just needed time alone to deal with the disappointment of getting so close only to watch the redemption he'd wanted slip through his fingers. She completely understood the decision he was making… but that didn't make it suck any less.

It was late at night when the plane touched down. They disembarked and Blakely tried not to worry about the fact that Gray kept his distance and didn't touch her. He was just dealing with things.

That was, until they reached the tarmac. Two cars waited for them. Blakely caught a glimpse of her bag being loaded into one…and Gray's being put into the other.

Turning, she said, "What's going on?"

"What do you mean?"

"Why are we taking separate cars?"

Gray cocked his head to the side. "Because we're both going home."

Blakely couldn't stop herself, even though she already knew the answer. "Alone?"

"Yes."

"Why?"

He pulled in a deep breath and held it for several seconds before finally letting it out. "Look, Blakely. You held up your end of the bargain. You helped me prove my innocence."

"Even though you're not going to do anything with the information."

His mouth thinned. "Even though. I'm following through with my end. You should be receiving a phone call tomorrow from an accounting firm in town. They're going to interview you, but it's just a formality. You can start your life and career over."

Blakely stared at Gray for several seconds. An anxious pit opened up in the bottom of her belly. This wasn't what she wanted.

"That's it?" Her purse slipped through numbed fingers, dropping to the ground at her feet. She took several steps forward, right into his personal space. Gray didn't flinch—he just stared at her out of cold, remote eyes.

This was not the man who'd rocked her world and spent hours worshipping her body just days ago. The man in front of her was the aloof felon. The intense brawler hell-bent on victory.

"You're going to pretend the last few days didn't happen? That you didn't spend hours with your mouth and hands on my body?"

"No, why would I pretend it didn't happen? I enjoyed every minute of it. You did, too. But that was just proximity and chemistry, Blakely. We were physically attracted to each other."

"Were." The single word fell flat.

"There's no reason for us to see each other again. The job is finished."

"What if I want to stay at Stone?" She'd really enjoyed the work they'd done together. Being part of solving the puzzle had been exhilarating. And it didn't hurt that they'd been trying to find justice, something she prized highly thanks to her childhood. Being part of that had felt...purposeful and important.

"I don't think that's a good idea."

"Why? You're not this asshole, Gray."

His mouth twisted into a self-deprecating smile. "I assure you, I can be as much an asshole as the next guy. It was fun while it lasted, but it's over. Time for both of us to go back to our lives."

Blakely stared up at him, a mixture of hurt, pride, anger and pain making her physically ill. Heat washed over her body, and not the kind that normally filled her when Gray was near. Her stomach felt like she'd swallowed a cup of battery acid.

She refused to beg him, even if her brain was screaming at her to convince him he was wrong. She deserved to be with a man who wanted her, not someone who felt she was disposable as soon as she wasn't useful to him anymore.

Never once had she thought Gray was that kind of man, but apparently, she was wrong.

Taking two steps back, Blakely began nodding her head. "Normal. That's exactly what I need."

She spun on her heel and stalked away. It was either that, or let him see the tears she couldn't hold back silently rolling down her face.

"What the hell is your problem? You've been a right prick the last few days." Finn leaned back in the large leather chair, a single dark eyebrow winged up in that sharp, insolent and questioning way he had.

Gray fought the urge to reach across the table and punch him. Logically, he realized the reaction was way too much. But he was having a very hard time controlling his temper.

"Heartbroken fool." Those two words were Stone's contribution to the conversation.

"O-o-oh," Finn said, drawing out the single word. "Poor bastard."

Stone shrugged. "He did it to himself so I don't have a lot of sympathy."

Finn's lips tipped up at the corners. "Yeah, but you remember both of us had a stupid moment ourselves before we got our heads out our asses."

"Speak for yourself. I don't remember any stupid moments."

Finn scoffed, the incredulous sound echoing through the room and scraping against his last nerve. "Bullshit. Just because you don't want to admit it, doesn't mean it didn't happen. Besides, I'm pretty sure you had more than one."

"No reason to go there," Stone said with a pointed look. "Besides, we were talking about Gray."

"Any bets on how long it takes before he comes to his senses, goes after her and grovels?"

Stone tipped his head sideways, studying him like he was a specimen beneath a microscope. "I'm pretty sure he's close to the breaking point right now. I'd say...two days. Max."

"Nah, I'm going with tomorrow. I hear her dad's case is going before the judge then."

"No fair, you had insider information."

Finn grinned. "Always stack the deck, my friend."

Gray, tired of listening to the banter, growled, "You assholes can stop talking about me like I'm not here."

"Well, look at that, he is paying attention."

"Of course I am." His attention turned to Finn. "Her father's trial is tomorrow?"

This time both of Finn's eyebrows rose. "The high-priced lawyer you hired filed a motion to dismiss. The judge is hearing it tomorrow. Although, I would have expected you to know this already."

And he might have...if he hadn't told the guy who'd called yesterday about Blakely's father's case that he didn't want to hear anything about it. He just wanted the man to do his job. Period.

Dammit, but now he knew. His foot started tapping against the floor. The muscles in his shoulders tightened. Blakely must be stressed out over the outcome.

He needed to get out of here, before he did something stupid. Like call her and see how she was holding up.

Pushing back from the table, Gray said, "You guys will have to finish this meeting without me."

"Please tell me you're going to her."

Gray looked across the table at Stone. "No."

His friend groaned, closing his eyes. "You really are a fool." Waving a hand, Stone added, "Go, we've got this. Do us a favor, though, and don't come back in until you have your shit together. Amanda is afraid to come near you right now. She said you snapped her head off when she brought you some paperwork this morning."

"It was screwed up."

"Maybe so, but that wasn't her fault."

Stone might be right, but Gray wasn't in the mood to acknowledge it. "Whatever."

He was halfway to the door when Finn's voice stopped him. "Would you like some friendly advice?"

Gray paused for several seconds before turning back to his friend. "Not really."

"You're getting it, anyway. I don't know what happened between you. What I do know is that with her you were happier than I'd ever seen you. And that's saying a lot considering everything that was going on. I would have expected the last few weeks to have been some of the most difficult of your life."

And when Gray stopped to think about it, Finn was right. Aside from being convicted for a crime he didn't commit, finding out his mother wasn't really his, that his father had paid someone to cover it up and his birth mother had sold him…not exactly a happy time.

"Still, somehow, you managed to get through that experience without tearing apart someone or something. I saw you smile more often in those weeks than I have in the eight years I've known you. She makes you happy, man. And that's worth a lot."

Stone picked up where Finn left off. "It's worth doing whatever you have to in order to have that in your life. Whatever the problem is…figure out how to fix it. All of us know, life is too unpredictable. You take the joy where you can find it."

"And when you find a woman worth having in your life, you do what you can to keep her there," Finn added.

Gray stared at both his friends. They watched him with matching earnest expressions, firmly believing what they were telling him.

And he had to admit, the last few days he'd been miserable.

"This is the right thing…for her. It'll get better."

"No, it won't," Stone said, his voice filled with certainty. "I let Piper go before I went to prison. And those feelings never disappeared. They were just as powerful years later. If you love her, tell her."

"Fight for her," Finn chimed in. "You're good at that, man. You know how to fight. So why are you walking away from the most important one of your life?"

Gray's gaze bounced between his two friends.

Aside from Blakely, they were the most important people in his life.

What they said both scared him…and gave him hope. Maybe they were right. Stone had been noble, trying to do the right thing just like he was. But in the end, Piper hadn't wanted that sacrifice from him. She'd wanted the man she loved.

Walking away from Blakely was the hardest thing he'd ever done. And Finn had a point. He'd never backed down from a fight before. So why was he doing it now, when it mattered most?

"That's a damn good question."

Fifteen

Blakely sat behind her father. He was at the table in front of her. The lawyer Gray had hired sat next to him. She'd half expected the guy to drop the case, but he hadn't.

She couldn't decide whether to be grateful or pissed. Half of her had hoped Gray would pull an asshole move so she could be angry instead of hurt and heartbroken.

No such luck.

The bastard.

The judge walked into the courtroom and everyone stood. After he was seated, the bailiff instructed everyone else to sit. The registrar began detailing the order of cases. The hearing for her father's motion was first.

Everyone was shuffling papers and murmuring. Getting prepared. Blakely's stomach was in knots. Over the last several days, she'd spent some time with her father, really talking about what had happened. A few weeks ago, she would have gone into that conversation with a completely different mindset. But thanks to Gray…she'd truly listened to her father and decided for herself, and for him, that she believed him. He was far from perfect, but it was clear to her he'd been honestly trying to change his life.

Which made this hearing even more important.

Leaning forward, Blakely placed her hand over her father's shoulder and squeezed. He didn't turn, but brought his own hand up, covering hers. The pads of his fingers were rough with calluses, reminding her that no matter what, her father had worked hard all of his life to provide for his family. Maybe not the way she would have preferred…but the only way he knew how.

The hearing started, and the prosecution began with a brief outline of their case. Blakely listened to the evidence, her throat tightening with each word. They made him sound so guilty.

The defense was about to start when the door at the back of the courtroom opened. Blakely turned at the noise, nothing more than a reflex, but her world stood still when she saw who entered.

Gray.

What was he doing here?

Pausing, he looked straight at her for several moments. His expression was blank and impossible to read. A jumbled mess of emotions tangled into knots inside her already rolling belly. Anger, heartbreak, hope and frustration collided, so coiled together that she couldn't separate them enough to deal with any.

Clamping her jaws together, Blakely purposefully turned away from him, placing her focus back onto her father and the hearing.

She listened to her father's attorney decimate each of the prosecution's points, poking holes in their evidence and making a strong case for dismissing the charges altogether. He also made a compelling argument that her father had been turning his life around, distancing himself from the people who were bad influences and attempting to become a better citizen. He suggested no one should be judged based on their past behavior when they were clearly trying to make the right changes.

The experience was a roller coaster, but optimistic hope came out on top when her father's attorney finally sat. And in that moment, she was proud of her father. Something she'd never been able to say before.

When both sides were done, the judge sat back in his chair. He looked out over the courtroom, his gaze zeroing in on her father.

"Mr. Whittaker, I've heard from both sides. After careful consideration of the facts presented here, I find there isn't enough evidence to hold this case over for trial."

Blakely let out a huge sigh of relief. In front of her, her father sagged into his chair, his shoulders dipping with relief.

"I want to caution you, however. While it might be ideal not to judge people on their past mistakes, ultimately, we're all human and it happens. You have much to atone for in your past, but I'm a firm believer everyone deserves a second chance. So far, you've proven your willingness to make changes in your life. Keep it that way so I don't have to see you in my courtroom again." The judge paused for several seconds. "Because next time, you might not be so lucky."

Her father stood. "Thank you, sir. I understand and I'm so grateful for your decision."

Everyone around her seemed to move at once. Her father's attorney stood and began gathering his files and papers. He turned to her father and murmured several things before clapping him on the back and wishing him the best.

Her father turned to her, a huge grin stretching across his face. Blakely leaned forward, wrapping him in a hug. But she couldn't stop herself from whispering in his ear. "You're lucky, Dad. Please don't blow this second chance."

"I won't, baby girl. I promise not to let you down again."

Pulling back, Blakely looked deep into his eyes. "Dad, don't do it for me. Do it for yourself."

The smile on Martin's face dimmed a little, but he nodded and squeezed her shoulder.

Together, they walked out of the courtroom. Blakely couldn't stop herself from scanning the crowd in front of her, looking for Gray even though she knew she shouldn't.

But he wasn't there.

And for some stupid reason, her heart dropped into her toes when she realized he was gone. He hadn't come for her; he'd come to support her father. To make sure his money had been spent wisely.

In that moment, the last bit of hope Blakely had been clinging to disappeared.

Gray watched as Blakely and her father left the courthouse. Martin got into his car and drove away. His daughter stood for several seconds, watching him disappear.

Her hands were shaking. He wanted to go to her, hold her, and make it stop.

She was so strong for everyone, but for the first time, Gray realized that meant she had no one to be strong for her.

No, that wasn't true. She had him.

To hell with it. He didn't care if she wanted him to be there or not. Didn't care if she was angry with him, or if she didn't like his criminal reputation. They'd figure it out.

Walking out of the shadows, Gray crossed the sidewalk. Reaching out, he grasped her hands and squeezed.

She didn't startle or jerk away. But she also didn't turn to him. Instead, she stared straight ahead and asked, "Why are you here?"

"I wouldn't be anywhere else."

Blakely's head bowed.

Using his grip on her shoulders, Gray gently

turned her to face him. Her face was drawn, unhappy and sad. Exactly the way he'd been feeling the past days without her.

"Blakely, I'm miserable without you." Those words were a hell of a lot easier to say than he'd expected. "I miss your laugh, the way you smell. I miss the way you burrow into me in your sleep, like you can't get close enough. I miss the way you argue with me and challenge me. I just miss you."

Blakely's mouth thinned. Her eyes glistened with tears she wouldn't let fall. "You pushed me away, Gray."

"You're right. I did. I was afraid."

"Of what?"

"That you were only with me out of guilt." No, it was more than that. And if there was ever a time to be completely honest with himself and her, it was now. "I was afraid I didn't deserve you. Blakely, I spent seven years in prison. And I might not have been a criminal when I went inside—"

Blakely cut him off, her voice hard and strong when she said, "You're still not a criminal."

And that was where she was wrong. "I've done plenty of things that are on the gray side of the law. And I know you, Blakely. If you knew everything, you wouldn't be okay with it."

"That's bullshit, Gray. You say you know me, but I know you, too. I don't care what you think you've done. I have no doubt you had perfectly good reasons. Period. I don't need the details to know that, because I know you. Trust you."

Blakely's arm flung out, sweeping across the expanse of the courthouse steps. "I just spent the last hour in a courtroom with my dad. A few weeks ago, dread and disappointment would have sat heavy on my stomach. Because I would have been embarrassed and hurt by what he'd done. Instead, I was hopeful. And not just because you'd spent money on a damn good lawyer. But because I believe that deep down, he wants to change. I believe in him, in a way I never have before. You gave me that." She shook her head. "No, you gave *us* that. Because my support is going to help my dad be successful in making those changes."

Gray's chest tightened. "I'm really happy for you both."

"Then why won't you let me show you the same support you've given me?"

Blakely closed the gap between them, wrapping her hands around his face and bringing her body snugly against his. "I love you, Gray."

Everything inside him went silent at her words. Something sharp lanced through his chest and then warmth expanded, spreading throughout his entire body.

She loved him. Gray wasn't certain what he'd done right in his life to deserve her, but he'd take it. Because he wasn't strong enough not to.

Dropping his forehead to hers, he said, "I love you, too."

"There might have been a time I thought you were the worst kind of man, but I was clearly wrong. Gray

Lockwood, you're one of the most honorable, selfless men I've ever met."

Gray's throat tight, he pulled her up until his mouth met hers. The kiss they shared was hot as always, but it was more. Connection, comfort, support and appreciation.

It was a beginning, one they were both anxious to start.

* * * * *

Don't miss any of the Bad Billionaires!

The Rebel's Redemption
The Devil's Bargain
The Sinner's Secret

WE HOPE YOU ENJOYED
THIS BOOK FROM

⟨H⟩ HARLEQUIN
DESIRE

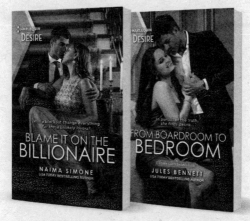

*Luxury, scandal, desire—welcome to
the lives of the American elite.*

Be transported to the worlds of oil barons, family dynasties,
moguls and celebrities. Get ready for juicy plot twists,
delicious sensuality and intriguing scandal.

6 NEW BOOKS AVAILABLE EVERY MONTH!

HDHALO2020

COMING NEXT MONTH FROM

♦ HARLEQUIN
DESIRE

Available December 1, 2020

#2773 THE WIFE HE NEEDS
Westmoreland Legacy: The Outlaws • by Brenda Jackson
Looking to settle down, Alaskan CEO Garth Outlaw thinks he wants
a convenient bride. What he doesn't know is that his pilot,
Regan Fairchild, wants *him*. Now, with two accidental weeks together in
paradise, will the wife he needs be closer than he realized?

#2774 TEMPTED BY THE BOSS
Texas Cattleman's Club: Rags to Riches • by Jules Bennett
The only way to get Kelly Prentiss's irresistible workaholic boss
Luke Holloway to relax is to trick him—into taking a vacation with her!
The island heat ignites a passion they can't ignore, but will it be back to
business once their getaway ends?

#2775 OFF LIMITS ATTRACTION
The Heirs of Hansol • by Jayci Lee
Ambitious Colin Song wants his revenge—by working with producer
Jihae Park. But remaining enemies is a losing battle with their sizzling
chemistry! Yet how can they have a picture-perfect ending when
everyone's secret motives come to light?

#2776 HOT HOLIDAY FLING
by Joss Wood
Burned before, the only thing businessman Hunt Sheridan wants is
a no-strings affair with career-focused Adie Ashby-Tate. When he
suggests a Christmas fling, it's an offer she can't refuse. But will their hot
holiday fantasy turn into a gift neither was expecting?

#2777 SEDUCING THE LOST HEIR
Clashing Birthrights • by Yvonne Lindsay
When identical twin Logan Harper learns he was stolen at birth, he vows
to claim the life he was denied. Until he's mistakenly seduced by
Honor Gould, *his twin's fiancée*! Their connection is undeniable, but
they're determined not to make the same mistake twice...

#2778 TAKING ON THE BILLIONAIRE
Redhawk Reunion • by Robin Covington
Tess Lynch once helped billionaire Adam Redhawk find his Cherokee
family. Now he needs her again—to find who's sabotaging his company.
But she has a secret agenda that doesn't stop sparks from flying. Will
the woman he can't resist be his downfall?

**YOU CAN FIND MORE INFORMATION ON UPCOMING HARLEQUIN TITLES,
FREE EXCERPTS AND MORE AT HARLEQUIN.COM.**

HDCNM1120

SPECIAL EXCERPT FROM

⊕HARLEQUIN

DESIRE

*Looking to settle down, Alaskan CEO Garth Outlaw
thinks he wants a convenient bride. What he doesn't
know is that his pilot, Regan Fairchild, wants him. Now,
with two accidental weeks together in paradise, will the
wife he needs be closer than he realized?*

Read on for a sneak peek at
The Wife He Needs
by New York Times *bestselling author Brenda Jackson.*

"May I go on record to make something clear, Regan?" Garth
asked, kicking off his shoes.

She swallowed. He was standing, all six feet and three inches
of him, at the foot of the bed, staring at her with the same intensity
that she felt. She wasn't sure what he had to say, but she definitely
wanted to hear it.

"Yes," she said in an almost whisper.

"You don't need me to make you feel sexy, desired and wanted.
You are those things already. What I intend to do is to make you feel
needed," he said, stepping away from the bed to pull his T-shirt over
his head and toss it on a nearby chair. "If you only knew the depth
of my need for you."

She wondered if being needed also meant she was indispensable,
essential, vital, crucial...all those things she wanted to become to
him.

"Now I have you just where I want you, Regan. In my bed."

And whether he knew it or not, she had him just where she
wanted him, too. Standing in front of her and stripping, for starters.
As she watched, his hands went to the front of his jeans.

"And I have you doing what I've always fantasized about, Garth.
Taking your clothes off in front of me so I can see you naked."

She could tell from the look on his face that her words surprised
him. "You used to fantasize about me?"

"All the time. You always looked sexy in your business suits, but my imagination gets a little more risqué than that."

He shook his head. "I never knew."

"What? That I wanted you as much as you wanted me? I told you that in the kitchen earlier."

"I assumed that desire began since you've been here with me."

Boy, was he wrong. "No, it goes back further than that."

It was important that he knew everything. Not only that the desire was mutual but also that it hadn't just begun. If he understood that then it would be easier for her to build the kind of relationship they needed, regardless of whether he thought they needed it or not.

"I never knew," he said, looking a little confused. "You never said anything."

"I wasn't supposed to. You are my boss and I am a professional."

He nodded because she knew he couldn't refute that. "How long have you felt that way?"

There was no way she would tell him that she'd had a crush on him since she was sixteen, or that he was the reason she had returned to Fairbanks after her first year in college. She had heard he was back home from the military with a broken heart, and she'd been determined to fix it. Things didn't work out quite that way. He was deep in mourning for the woman he'd lost and had built a solid wall around himself, one that even his family hadn't been able to penetrate for a long while.

"The length of time doesn't matter, Garth. All you need to know is that the desire between us is mutual. Now, are you going to finish undressing or what?"

Don't miss what happens next in...
The Wife He Needs
by Brenda Jackson, the first book in her
Westmoreland Legacy: The Outlaws series!

Available November 2020 wherever
Harlequin Desire books and ebooks are sold.

Harlequin.com

Copyright © 2020 by Brenda Streater Jackson

HDEXP1120

Get 4 FREE REWARDS!

We'll send you 2 FREE Books plus 2 FREE Mystery Gifts.

Harlequin Desire® books transport you to the world of the American elite with juicy plot twists, delicious sensuality and intriguing scandal.

FREE Value Over **$20**

YES! Please send me 2 FREE Harlequin Desire novels and my 2 FREE gifts (gifts are worth about $10 retail). After receiving them, if I don't wish to receive any more books, I can return the shipping statement marked "cancel." If I don't cancel, I will receive 6 brand-new novels every month and be billed just $4.55 per book in the U.S. or $5.24 per book in Canada. That's a savings of at least 13% off the cover price! It's quite a bargain! Shipping and handling is just 50¢ per book in the U.S. and $1.25 per book in Canada.* I understand that accepting the 2 free books and gifts places me under no obligation to buy anything. I can always return a shipment and cancel at any time. The free books and gifts are mine to keep no matter what I decide.

225/326 HDN GNND

Name (please print)

Address   Apt. #

City   State/Province   Zip/Postal Code

Email: Please check this box ☐ if you would like to receive newsletters and promotional emails from Harlequin Enterprises ULC and its affiliates. You can unsubscribe anytime.

Mail to the **Reader Service:**
IN U.S.A.: P.O. Box 1341, Buffalo, NY 14240-8531
IN CANADA: P.O. Box 603, Fort Erie, Ontario L2A 5X3

Want to try 2 free books from another series? Call 1-800-873-8635 or visit www.ReaderService.com.

*Terms and prices subject to change without notice. Prices do not include sales taxes, which will be charged (if applicable) based on your state or country of residence. Canadian residents will be charged applicable taxes. Offer not valid in Quebec. This offer is limited to one order per household. Books received may not be as shown. Not valid for current subscribers to Harlequin Desire books. All orders subject to approval. Credit or debit balances in a customer's account(s) may be offset by any other outstanding balance owed by or to the customer. Please allow 4 to 6 weeks for delivery. Offer available while quantities last.

Your Privacy—Your information is being collected by Harlequin Enterprises ULC, operating as Reader Service. For a complete summary of the information we collect, how we use this information and to whom it is disclosed, please visit our privacy notice located at corporate.harlequin.com/privacy-notice. From time to time we may also exchange your personal information with reputable third parties. If you wish to opt out of this sharing of your personal information, please visit readerservice.com/consumerchoice or call 1-800-873-8635. **Notice to California Residents**—Under California law, you have specific rights to control and access your data. For more information on these rights and how to exercise them, visit corporate.harlequin.com/california-privacy.

HD20R2

Love Harlequin romance?

DISCOVER.

Be the first to find out about promotions, news and exclusive content!

 Facebook.com/HarlequinBooks

Twitter.com/HarlequinBooks

Instagram.com/HarlequinBooks

Pinterest.com/HarlequinBooks

ReaderService.com

EXPLORE.

Sign up for the Harlequin e-newsletter and download a free book from any series at **TryHarlequin.com**

CONNECT.

Join our Harlequin community to share your thoughts and connect with other romance readers!
Facebook.com/groups/HarlequinConnection

HSOCIAL2020